Dakota

Sarah Patt

Dakota

Addison & Highsmith

Addison & Highsmith Publishers

Las Vegas ◊ Chicago ◊ Palm Beach

Published in the United States of America by
Histria Books
7181 N. Hualapai Way, Ste. 130-86
Las Vegas, NV 89166 USA
HistriaBooks.com

Addison & Highsmith is an imprint of Histria Books. Titles published under the imprints of Histria Books are distributed worldwide.

Library of Congress Control Number: 2021940157

ISBN 978-0-9801164-3-4 (hardcover)
ISBN 978-1-59211-277-7 (softbound)
ISBN 978-1-59211-279-1 (eBook)

Dedication

This book is dedicated to my devoted and loving husband,
Michael, and our adult children, Zachary, Benjamin, and Olivia
who will always be "my babies". ;) Your gourmet meals, baked
goodies, game nights, and fitness regimes were my salvation. I
am forever grateful and love you all beyond measure.

Chapter 1

The Wedding

"OH, AMBER LEE, you look beautiful," I cooed, smiling at her gorgeousness, pleasantly surprised her billowing gown didn't dwarf her petite frame. Atop her loose strawberry-blonde hair, a delicate floral wreath was perfectly placed. "You truly look like a fairy tale princess."

She spoke to my reflection in the cheval mirror. "Thank you, Dakota. And thank you so much for offering me your mother's wedding veil as my 'something borrowed.'"

"You're very welcome. My mom would be happy you're wearing it. She would've loved you."

Feeling sentimental, Amber Lee dabbed at the corners of her eyes with a tissue before any tears could smudge her mascara.

Our tender moment was interrupted by a knock at the door, followed by a cheerful voice.

"Is my beautiful daughter ready yet to have her daddy walk her down the aisle?"

"Dad, you can come in," Amber Lee answered. "I'm as ready as I'll ever be."

"Dear Lord. Aren't you a vision! You're as beautiful as your mother was forty years ago."

Amber Lee smiled.

"You have her face and frame. But your mother didn't show as much cleavage. Can you pull it up?" he said as he mimicked the act on himself. "They're bustin' out!"

"DAD!" Amber Lee blushed. "That isn't what a father asks his daughter, especially on her wedding day!"

Amber Lee looked mortified as she pulled up the bustier and then pushed down on her bosoms as if this would flatten them. I was laughing, also surprised Mr. Brickman actually said that, but it was true. Amber Lee was ending her first trimester, so, naturally, her breasts were filling out. As for her belly — she wore a girdle that hid it. When she asked me to be her maid of honor, she confided that she was pregnant, but I knew. It doesn't take a brain surgeon to figure out why a bride was getting married within three months of getting engaged.

"Oh, not to worry — the veil will hide it. Now turn around," I told her as I gently placed the front of the long, sheer headdress over her face and chest. "Beautiful — can't see a thing. But my brother will blush once he lifts it to kiss his new wife!"

She smiled.

"All right, ladies," Mr. Brickman said as he gestured to his daughter for her to take hold of his crooked arm, "Shall we?"

We could hear the music had begun. I opened the doors of our prep room and led us to the church's foyer, where the ring bearer (Amber Lee's nephew, Timmy) and the flower girl (Luke's daughter, Savannah) were restlessly waiting with the wedding coordinator. Timmy looked adorable. It was my first time seeing a small child wearing a tux. Of course, Savannah looked precious, too, in her fancy mauve taffeta dress. The coordinator smiled and opened the doors of the chapel. The fanfare began. The ring bearer and flower girl started their walk. As the first strains of "The Wedding March" began, I followed slowly. Each pew was delicately embellished with fragrant sprigs of lily of the valley. Like most grooms, Luke stood with folded hands and excellent posture beside the best man, Uncle Travis, who held the same stance. When I came to my standstill spot on the altar, I noticed a bit of perspiration forming on Luke's forehead. There was nothing for him to be nervous about. Perhaps he was just warm in the rented tux and felt uncomfortable in this formal attire — Luke was as casual as they come. He would have preferred a more laid-back ceremony, outside under a tree, followed by a Texan BBQ, especially since this was his second marriage. But it was Amber Lee's first and 'only' nuptials. She had always dreamed of getting married in the church she was brought up in, followed by a fancy three-course dinner reception afterward at the country club she was also familiar with. However, the formal ballroom was already booked and paid for as well as the other, less formal banquet hall the club usually used for award ceremonies, so the third-best choice would be to have the reception in the backyard of the house where she was raised, which was just as stately as any country club. Then Luke winked at me, and I knew all was good.

All heads turned to see Amber Lee come down the aisle. All but my boyfriend, who was giving me a blatant invitation — his sensual gaze raking mercilessly over my figure. He stood beside my best friend, Gloria, who was holding hands with her boyfriend, Cooper, who had secretly confessed he loved me not too long ago. Naturally, I was taken aback and brushed it off, thinking he was confusing our commonalities — our having lost both our parents and perhaps he took advantage of my vulnerability. At the time, I was still shaken up over the freak hit-and-run accident involving my uncle, who was with his girlfriend, Pamela, in a taxi, and Jake Jennings. Jake rammed into their taxi with his Cadillac Escalade and killed the driver. Needless to say, both thoughts were weighing on my mind.

I stood at the altar, trying to pay attention, but couldn't help think what would happen when my boyfriend left for med school in Connecticut — two thousand miles from Texas. Coincidentally, my best friend was also headed to Yale for undergrad. I'd be left behind in Houston studying at Rice University, which wasn't far from where Cooper lived. Would he pop by and repeat those three words to me? Would I be able to suppress my true feelings?

Chapter 2

Dr. Cavanaugh

THE GUESTS made their way to the large veranda where champagne and hors d'oeuvres were being served. I steered to the slate patio where two bars were on either end and planted myself on one of the barstools, letting my high heels fall off.

I was holding my right foot, trying to massage the soreness out of it, when Hubbell's dad, Dr. Cavanaugh, approached.

"What seems to be the trouble, Dakota?" he asked, in an aristocratic voice that made me cringe every time he spoke.

What the heck does it look like, idiot? My foot hurts! was what I really felt like saying, but instead, I answered, "My horse stepped on it." Then I decided to get his goat and added, "Besides, don't sore feet come with pregnancy?"

Dr. Cavanaugh looked like I had punched him in the gut. It was the most outright look of surprise I'd ever seen on his face. It took him a minute to gather himself enough to say, "I'm sorry, Dakota."

I was not expecting Dr. Cavanaugh to apologize — a grown man admitting to a teenager he was wrong. Back in January, when I found out Hubbell was going to Yale Medical School, I was hurt, but only because it was kept from me. I found out through Gloria because she had overheard Dr. Cavanaugh bragging about his son going to his alma mater. So when Hubbell and I got into our first fight, he went home teary-eyed, and his overprotective, self-righteous dad phoned me to explain, but instead, warned me not to do anything that would jeopardize his son's future, like trapping him with a baby, which I would never, ever do.

"Huh?" I said with furrowed brows. "You're actually apologizing? So you know how out of line you were?"

He gave a pursed smile, took out his tortoise-rimmed glasses from the inner breast pocket of his pinstriped suit, and put them on. He then took my aching foot with a light touch of his hands to examine it. I felt warmth in my heart. It was at that moment I could see where Hubbell inherited his tenderness from.

"Glad it isn't the injured leg," he said.

I was surprised he remembered which leg of mine was in a cast a few months ago. It was the outcome of my uncle's hit and run accident. The perpetrator, Jake Jennings of Jennings Petroleum — my dad's employer of twenty-plus years, hid his vehicle in the garage of my former, desolate home in Fort Worth. I went there to retrieve my mother's wedding veil for Amber Lee and search through some boxes in the attic for childhood photos of my dad because I was creating a surprise slide show for Luke. When Jennings learned of this somehow, he showed up late at night unannounced. He actually came through the garage door he had opened with the remote he had stolen some time ago. I instinctively hid — under my bed, but it didn't save me — Jennings had pulled me out and pinned me down. He was mildly inebriated, belligerent, and incredibly strong. If it weren't for my busybody neighbor, Mrs. Angela Turner, knocking on the front door, hollering, "What's all the commotion?" who knows what Jennings would have done to me. He stood hidden from view, pointing his gun at the front door, and told me to get rid of her. As much as Mrs. Turner looked like a sweet old lady, she was ornery and wouldn't succumb to my shooing her away with some lame excuse, like the screaming came from a horror movie I was watching on TV. No. It was the cut I got from Jennings slapping me across the face to shut me up that got her attention. His big-ass college ring had sliced my cheek, and old Mrs. Turner had turned into Florence Nightingale in mere seconds. She pushed her way in and practically ordered me to get the first aid kit. I lied and told her I had tripped and fallen on something sharp in the attic while looking for my mom's wedding veil. She insisted I make us a pot of tea and then tried to convince me I was too young to get married, even though I had explained minutes prior who the veil was for. It was then I remembered Mrs. Turner was also a little senile. When she had finished her second cup of tea, I politely repeated how I really needed to go to bed. She finally consented to leave but needed to use my bathroom first. Jennings then reappeared, standing right behind me, warning me not to try anything stupid, startling the shit out of me. I yelped, nearly dropping Mrs. Turner's teacup I was cleaning. At that precise moment, the old lady shot out of the bathroom with fire in her eyes and a can of Lysol in her hand and sprayed it into his eyes like there was no tomorrow! Impulsively he covered his eyes with both his hands, rubbing them clear, and stumbled back while I quickly grabbed my mom's casserole dish and smashed it on his head! My mobile phone was dead, and the landline had been shut off, so Mrs. Turner told me to run to her house and call 911. As I was fleeing the scene, he became cognizant and quickly took aim, shooting me in the leg. If it weren't for Mrs. Turner hitting him on the head with my mom's cast iron pan, he might have shot at me again. She gave herself a heart attack, hoisting that heavy pan, and I imagined her saying, "*Hasta la vista, baby!*" Although I doubt she ever watched those Arnold Schwarzenegger movies, in my mind, at that life-threatening moment, she *was* the Terminator! and I'll never forget her as long as I live.

Dr. Cavanaugh kept his head tilted down as his dark eyes looked up at me. Through the edge of his spectacles, which were now resting lower on his nose, he gave his diagnosis with sincerity in his voice.

"Looks a bit swollen, Dakota, and there's definitely a bruise forming. I don't think there's a break, but if it gets worse, you should get it x-rayed — there could be what's called a hairline fracture. Again, when did this happen?"

"Three days ago. I wanted to get a ride in before we had to leave for Atlanta. I was sandwiched between Christmas and his stall's opening."

Dr. Brickman interrupted, "Let me guess, it was Christmas when you got this horse?"

I nodded.

"How original."

I ignored his facetiousness and continued, "When I was steering Christmas and patting his rump, telling him what a good boy he was — he stepped on my foot."

"Hmm. I've never been into horses … or any animal, for that matter. I don't understand the fascination some people have with them."

I didn't respond to such a ludicrous statement. The thought of my Hubbell growing up without a pet made me sad. "It didn't hurt then as much as it does now. I'm sure the three-inch heels aren't helping any."

"No, they aren't. The shoes are making it worse — don't wear them. Your dress will cover your cute little toes," he remarked playfully, wiggling a toe of mine.

I thought he was going to start, 'this little piggy went to market.' Thank God he didn't — that would've been weird and embarrassing. He eased my foot back down. I was grateful for his unsolicited expertise, but I still didn't trust him. And I found him to be very moody. As Dr. Cavanaugh returned his eyeglasses to his breast pocket, he pulled out an envelope. "Oh, I almost forgot. Do Luke and Amber Lee have a money box — you know, where guests can slip in cards with the wedding moola?" he asked without looking at me.

He waved the envelope to get the bartender's attention, who was pouring champagne into a dozen fluted glasses on a silver tray as the server patiently waited.

"Be right with you, sir," the bartender said with a smile, looking up for a split second before filling the next glass. Dr. Cavanaugh called out anyway, "Two whiskey sours" without saying please. I quickly shook my head no. "Just one, please." It sounded like a gross cocktail.

"Huh?" Dr. Cavanaugh said, giving me a puzzled look that made me feel like I was stupid. "It's not for you, Dakota. It's for the missus."

The bartender shot me a look, inferring, 'This guy's a jerk.' Then with a forced smile, he said, "Two whiskey sours coming up, sir."

"I saw a gift table in the foyer," I answered, then, with a hint of sass, added, "Where you can stuff it."

Again, he didn't say thank you to the bartender or even a simple goodbye to me as he got up and walked away, carrying a tumbler in each hand and calling out what sounded like, "Be good!"

Chapter 3

Hubbell

"THERE YOU ARE," Hubbell said as he moved closer, kissed me, then positioned himself on the vacant barstool — still warm from his father. The bartender asked him what he'd like.

He answered with his usual, "Vodka tonic with an olive."

Hubbell always fed me the olive, whispering, "Olive you." He then eyed my bare feet.

"Your dad said I could get away with it. What do you think?"

"What, no shoes?" he replied playfully.

"Yeah. They kill."

"Go barefoot. No one will care."

When the bartender served Hubbell his drink, he looked at me and said, "And for the lady?"

Hubbell answered for me. "She'll have the same."

But what I really wanted was...

"May I get two Bud Lights please?" Cooper interrupted.

That! I really wanted a cold beer. And at that instant, a tinge of jealousy overcame me — I knew Cooper was ordering the second Bud Light for Gloria.

Hubbell and I both turned.

"Hi!"

Gloria glided in. "Wasn't that the most beautiful ceremony ever? Their vows were so romantic — makes me want to get married just so I could hear those words."

Gloria often exaggerated.

"I liked the *Letter To The Hebrews* the best," Cooper said, and winked at me. But deep down, I knew Cooper meant it as a genuine compliment. From the few books I'd read on coping with grief, a person who experiences tragedy either forfeits their belief in God or embraces it. And since Cooper lost both his parents when he was a teenager, he felt he needed the Lord more than ever.

The four of us clinked our glasses as I toasted, "To my incredible brother and his equally incredible wife."

"And to Yale!" Hubbell added, and Gloria agreed, "Yes. To Yale!"

Then Gloria kissed Cooper and Hubbell leaned in to kiss me. I was taken aback and turned my head, so his lips grazed my cheek. My sweet moment and selfless toast got bulldozed. I didn't toast to Rice University, so why should he toast to Yale? It was the first time he didn't feed me his olive, and I pretended not to notice when he ate it. Suddenly, music and a catchy song blared across the lawn. It was apparent that the band wanted to get everyone on the dance floor.

Gloria shrieked, "I love this song. Let's dance!"

Cooper, lifting his glass to his mouth, responded, "Let me finish my beer first."

Hubbell downed his drink and practically shouted, "I'll dance with you!"

"Awesome!" Gloria yelled as she took hold of Hubbell's hand, and the two of them shimmied to the dance floor.

"He can be such an idiot," Cooper commented.

"Yeah? How so?" I asked, trying to sound like I didn't know what he meant.

"You know, Dakota," he said, with flatness in his voice, as he stealthily took the miniature plastic sword from my vodka tonic and fed me the olive.

Without hesitation, I opened my mouth as if I were some pathetic, stray kitten he was feeding a morsel of salmon to. I stared into his gorgeous eyes and, as gingerly as I could, slid the olive off with my tongue.

"You were toasting to your family," he continued, "and Hubbell wanted it to be about him. Like always."

I remained speechless as he placed the empty sword on my cocktail napkin. For a moment, I imagined fencing with these tiny swords like a game of thumb wars. Cooper took a sip of his beer, swallowed, and turned to me, with gazing, serious eyes, "You deserve better, Dakota."

"Like you. I deserve you. That's really what you're trying to say... isn't it, Cooper?" I didn't let him answer. I finished my drink, said thank you again to the bartender, and hastily brushed past Cooper. He grasped my arm and said, "Yes," not letting me go. I froze. I wanted us to be alone like we were in my old home. When I had visited it to retrieve my mom's wedding veil, my car had broken down. It was providence that Cooper was also driving on the interstate and spotted me. After the tow truck hauled my car away, Cooper drove me the rest of the way.

I wanted us to kiss... like we had in my old home. We just stared into each other's eyes, which felt like an eternity until I heard my name being loudly called. The lead singer of the band was announcing me — the maid of honor. It was time for me to make my speech.

For a brief moment, I had forgotten where I put my speech and tried not to panic. The giddy feeling a first cocktail can bring on an empty stomach was running through my blood. I felt like a balloon free of its string. I took the microphone the DJ handed me, then miraculously, I remembered. With quick assurance and not acting the least bit embarrassed, I slipped the little piece of paper from my bra, which caused everyone to laugh. I needed two hands to unfold it, so I slipped the mic into my armpit — more laughter. I smiled. "Okay, I'm ready!" I joked. The photographer snapped at least ten shots. I had decided to keep my speech short and simple.

"Quoting the renowned French author, Antoine de Saint-Exupéry, 'Love does not consist in gazing at each other, but in looking together in the same direction.'" I looked towards where Amber Lee and Luke were seated at a large round table draped in cream linen with a crystal candelabra in the center, surrounded by a plethora of bud vases filled with blooming pink roses. "To my incredible brother Luke and his beautiful bride, Amber Lee, who is as beautiful on the inside as she is on the outside." Amber Lee's eyes were glossy. "May your life together be as full as the love that binds you at this moment, and may every day be as special as you two are to me. I love you both so much."

Cheers broke out as Luke and Amber Lee lifted their champagne flutes simultaneously, and Luke cooed, "We love you, too, baby." Then it was Uncle Travis' turn to give his speech as best man.

"I'm not sure if y'all know how Luke and I met," he started, pausing for a second, searching for the words he was going to say next.

He didn't have a cheat sheet like I had, and it sounded as if he was winging it.

"It was tragic," he blurted, shaking his head. "Devastating, actually."

It quickly grew quiet, and I prayed my uncle was going somewhere positive with this — very soon!

He continued. "It was unbelievable, but at the same time, spiritual. See, his father, Jethro, and I were best friends — more like brothers, really. And we told each other everything, but neither one of us knew Luke existed."

There was uncomfortable laughter. Guests shifted in their seats, grabbed their glasses for a sip, coughed, and cleared their throats.

"If Jethro knew he had a son, I don't think he could have done a better job raising him."

The guests cooed at this charming reference to Luke's late mother, Geraldine. Someone my uncle knew and didn't like but still acknowledged that in the end, she did well bringing up Luke. She had broken Jethro's heart by abruptly breaking up with him without offering a mature explanation and moved away, knowing she was carrying his child. She chose to raise Luke alone and did not divulge who the father was until she was dying. Tragically, it was too late — as Luke was on his way to Fort Worth to introduce himself as Jethro's long-lost son, he stopped for gas and noticed the headline of the local newspaper, FATAL ACCIDENT AT JENNING'S PETROLEUM. Within mere seconds of skimming the article, he saw the victim's name... Jethro Theodore Buchannan.

"In so many ways, Luke is like his father." Then pausing, added, "It's damn frightening."

The room filled with laughter.

"I may have lost my best friend, but I gained a new one... his son."

Then Uncle Travis lifted his old-fashioned glass. "May Luke and Amber Lee have an incredible life together and make a dozen babies."

The guests cheered, and the band played another popular dance song, slowly elevating the volume. Within seconds, guests pushed back their chairs and flooded the dance floor. The flower girl, Savannah, charged at Uncle Travis and me, grabbing our hands, and we swung her around, laughing. No matter how conflicting my feelings for Hubbell and Cooper were, I wasn't going to let it ruin my having fun at my brother's wedding.

Chapter 4

Drunk

WITHIN MINUTES after the band took a break, my consumption of alcohol began to take its toll. Rushing past other wedding guests to the nearest bathroom, I was greeted by Miss Ellie.

"Oh, Dakota, how many drinks have you had?"

The older and wiser woman, sensing the inevitable was coming, led me to the powder room, shut the door, took hold of my long locks, and held them away from my face as I hurled into the toilet.

"Oh, child, you ought to know better. The drink's the devil!" Miss Ellie scolded, but then with a deep sigh, said, gently patting my back, "There, there, child. You feeling better?"

I nodded, wiped my mouth with the back of my hand, and said, "Thank you."

"Of course."

She let go of my hair, walked a few steps to the sink, and wet a paper guest towel. She squeezed the excess water from it to blot my sweaty forehead, repeating, "There, there, child."

That was something my own mother would do. I uttered another "Thank you." I now felt a whole lot better. Then Gloria barged in, just as drunk as I was, and hurried to the toilet.

Gloria collapsed to her knees as I pushed myself over, still sitting on the floor but leaning against the wall. I held the cool towel against my forehead.

Miss Ellie hastily repositioned herself to make room for Gloria. Then she stood firmly with both hands fisted on her hips and scolded, "You girls ought to be ashamed of yourselves!"

Gloria hurled and then uttered, "OY!" as she rolled her eyes to me.

"Well, I got to tinkle!" Miss Ellie declared, "but seeing that I can't," she continued, staring down at Gloria with squinty, disapproving eyes. "I got to find myself another bathroom. So if you'll excuse me, girls, I'll let you be."

And before I could nod and say sorry and thank you again, she was out the door, shutting it with a purposeful bang.

"Who the heck was that lady?" Gloria cried. "And tinkle? What is she, two?"

I laughed but quickly came to Miss Ellie's defense, getting up and locking the bathroom door before anyone else could barge in. "That lady is Amber Lee's godmother — Miss Ellie May Washington. She's an incredible woman."

Gloria nodded, then turned to the toilet and puked one last time. I handed her my towel, and she wiped her mouth, declaring, "Oh, I feel so much better."

I eyed the carefully arranged basket of toiletries placed on a small antique pedestal table by the full-length mirror and rooted around for a breath mint. "Bingo!" I said as I took the roll of LifeSavers and popped a purple one into my mouth.

"This is some palatial powder room," Gloria admired, taking in the textured floral wallpaper and examining the tulip-shaped gilded sconces on either side of the mirror. "These are so cool, aren't they?"

I nodded. "Do you think the Cavanaugh's found those or the wallpaper first?"

"I'm guessing the lights first... then came the paper," Gloria answered, laughing at our chicken and egg analogy while washing her hands. "I feel guilty taking another one of these gorgeous monogrammed towels. They're the sturdiest paper towels I've ever seen. Feel 'em. They could pass as fabric." And then, with a laugh, she asked rhetorically, "Do you think they got these first, or the faucets first?"

I admired the oversized curlicued 'B' in gold and eased Gloria's guilt. "Don't toss it yet — I'll use it to dry my hands, too," I instructed as I squirted some liquid soap into my palm. "Ah, this smells like roses. Even the wastebasket is shaped like a tulip!" I said as I discarded the paper towel.

After we finished freshening ourselves up, we reentered the stately foyer. I couldn't help but think how fortunate Amber Lee was to have grown up in such a beautiful home and remain so humble. Her parents might be lushes, but they were kind and open-minded. Amber Lee was refined but not pretentious and a wonderful addition to the family. I felt truly blessed.

In a matter of seconds, our boys surprised us. Hubbell immediately took hold of me, wrapped his arms around my waist, and kissed me. Cooper playfully captured Gloria from behind. She gave out a shriek, followed by laughter. They whisked us back to the dance floor, and as soon as my bare toes hit the floor, a slow song began to play. Thank goodness, because I was too exhausted and in no mood for a fast dance. I rested my head on Hubbell's shoulder. His hands moved to the bridge of my behind and stayed there as his breath warmed my neck. I foolishly opened my eyes and felt Cooper's eyes on me. He saw me look at him. I quickly closed them again.

After the dance, it was back to the bar, but Gloria and I stuck with water while the boys drank some more.

Cooper began, "My grandparents give me their beach house in Rockport, Massachusetts for a week every summer. I usually start my week after spending my brother's last weekend with him and his family. I watch their kids so TJ and Linda can go out and enjoy a quiet, romantic dinner."

"You are so incredible," Gloria enthused.

"So I was wondering if y'all would like to fly to Boston, and I'll bring you out to the most charming New England town there is." I couldn't help but think how romantic it would be to spend a week with Hubbell by the sea.

Gloria immediately cried, "I'm in!"

Hubbell agreed, "Why not?"

I nodded my head and repeated Hubbell's, "Why not!"

"All right! I'll let you know as soon as I know what week exactly. It'll be awesome," Cooper said, his smile going from ear to ear. And the four of us toasted, "To Rockport!"

The wedding reception didn't end until two o'clock in the morning. I couldn't share a hotel room with Hubbell. I stayed at the Brickman's rather than at the nearby, inexpensive but clean Best Western, where all the guests were staying, including Gloria and Cooper. Of course, Gloria's parents assumed Gloria was staying with me. I was stuck with Amber Lee's lush of a mother, her overzealous dad, and Miss Page, the housekeeper.

Miss Page, with her beady eyes, didn't scare me. I considered it endearing when she bossed me around the day I had arrived — convincing me to help with the daily chores. Naturally, I obliged. I even told her how sweet I thought she was but purposely acted dumb just to get her goat.

"Is this the soap?" I asked as I held up the Palmolive. For some reason, she had thought I was born with a silver spoon in my mouth — privileged, with servants and never washing a pan in my short life.

She chortled and said, "Stop your foolin', Miss Dakota and scrub that pot 'till it shines like the top of the Chrysler building!"

I laughed, finding it ironic that she was quoting from Annie to little orphan Dakota. "Yes, Miss Hannigan!" I shot back, which went right over her head.

Up until the wedding night, Amber Lee shared her childhood bedroom with Savannah and me. Mr. Brickman lugged the rollaway bed from the attic and tried to set it up without our help, declaring he had it under control. But we had to save him before his fingers got pinched for the umpteenth time. It took all three of us to do it — crying to Savannah,

"Quickly, hop on!" as we latched the hinges — securing the creaky old cot when her weight plummeted onto it.

Afterward, Mr. Brickman huffed, "That calls for a drink."

And Amber Lee had looked at her watch and said, "Dad, it's only noon."

"Well, it's happy hour somewhere," he said as he shuffled out of the room. "See you downstairs for lunch."

I smirked, and Amber Lee rolled her eyes. "No wonder my mother's a lush — she's got a drinkin' buddy for a husband."

Then Savannah asked, "What's happy hour?"

Amber Lee chuckled and skirted the correct answer by declaring, "Every hour with you, my little cupcake, is happy hour!" Then she tickled Savannah in the ribs.

Just the sound of her infectious giggle relieved Amber Lee.

Chapter 5

Memorial Day Weekend

COOPER PHONED ME. I hadn't spoken to him since the wedding.

"Hey, Dakota. How've you been?"

"Great! What's up?"

"Remember when I told you my grandparents give me their Rockport home every year?"

"Uh-huh."

"Well, I know I said it'd be sometime in the summer, but their plans to go there over Memorial Day weekend changed and they offered it to me. So what do you say — do you want to head there at the end of May?"

It would be the one-year anniversary of my father's death, and a good distraction. I imagined he wouldn't want me sulking at home. "Sure. But what does Gloria think?" I asked, assuming he'd asked her first.

"Don't know yet. Thought I'd ask you first."

What? I thought. My heart skipped a beat. He didn't just say that. Gloria should get precedence. I reminded him assertively, "Cooper, Gloria's your girlfriend. Not me. You should call her and ask her!" I didn't give him a chance to rebut. My hands shaking, I blurted, "I've got to go. Bye," and hung up.

I hugged my bed pillow and cried. Cooper really did make me crazy. What was going to happen when Hubbell left for Connecticut and I stayed behind in Texas? I assured myself I'd keep busy to keep me distracted from missing Hubbell with every extra-curricular activity Rice University offered on top of the regular college load. I wondered if Cooper would put in longer hours at his ad agency to avoid thinking about Gloria as she began her freshman year at Yale. I questioned whether Hubbell and Gloria would even have time to meet up. I had heard the first week of medical school was the hardest, and the first assignment was to dissect a cadaver. I wondered if Hubbell was capable of cutting into a dead body without puking and passing out.

The thought of Cooper and me hooking up was always in the back of my mind. I'd read articles in Cosmopolitan magazine geared to relationships. However, the advice to stay faithful wasn't all that helpful nor encouraging. One article referred to the college years as "wild and free." Other advice columns considered this period of youth under the adage, 'the world is your oyster — do with it as you wish.' Why did Shakespeare ever compare being young, beautiful, and affluent with an ugly-looking bivalve?

Within minutes after Cooper phoned, Gloria called and sounded excited.

"Dakota, Cooper wants us to fly to Boston for Memorial Day weekend and party in Rockport! His grandparents are giving us their home. They sound so cool." Then her cheerful voice softened, sounding disappointed, "Although, I haven't met them yet."

I wondered why Cooper still hadn't made arrangements for her to meet his grandparents, considering they didn't live far from her in Fort Worth, and when he visited her, he stayed with them. A few times, he had stayed with them without making it a point to see her — supposedly, his excuse was that there wasn't enough time. When Cooper's parents were killed in a car accident, his maternal grandparents were made legal guardians of him and his older brother, TJ, who was deaf. There was a strong bond between Cooper and his grandparents that Gloria couldn't seem to nudge her way into.

"What do you say? Do you think you and Hubbell can make it?"

She didn't give me a chance to answer before she cooed, "It wouldn't be the same without you guys."

"Thanks, Gloria. I'm in, and I'm sure Hubbell can make it, too. I assume you're going to come here so the four of us can fly out of Houston together? I'll ask Luke if he can take us to the airport."

"Sounds like a plan. But first, I've gotta go convince my parents."

I guffawed, "What? You haven't told them yet?"

"Wish me luck!"

"Good luck!" and she was gone.

I was grateful my brother was cool and trusting — always saying I'd know the right decision to make in compromising situations. Whatever that meant. I often wondered how my life would have been different with my doting and overprotective parents — they'd never let me do half of what Luke okays.

Shortly after Gloria's phone call came Hubbell's. By the sound of his voice, you'd think he was the first one Cooper called about Rockport. I was annoyed at Hubbell's pretentiousness yet pretended this was the first I was hearing of the plan. While Hubbell rambled on with excitement about the trip, I mentally replayed Cooper's and my chance meeting in Fort Worth.

When I had driven to Fort Worth to retrieve my mother's wedding veil for Amber Lee, my car broke down on the interstate. Miraculously, Cooper spotted me on the side of the road. He was on his way to Dallas to visit his grandparents. He took me to my old home, and I stupidly invited him in — well, I asked him if he needed to use the bathroom, which he jumped on. After a short while, I felt overwhelmed by the memories in the house and fainted. Just like I had at my dad's funeral when Uncle Travis introduced me to Luke — the brother I didn't know I had. Cooper carried me to the sofa, placed a pillow under my head and a blanket over my body, and stayed with me until I woke up. He reminded me again how we had a lot in common — having both lost our parents. A strong emotional bond took over, and the next thing I knew, we were kissing. "I love you, Dakota,"

Cooper whispered, pushing back a strand of my hair with the gentle touch of his hand. Then he left.

Since that day, I found myself thinking about him. As much as Cooper made me crazy, he turned me on, and, as weird as it sounds, he was beginning to grow on me.

If this was one of those compromising situations about which Luke assured me I'd know the right decision to make, he was dead wrong. My mother used to say, "Even the smallest decisions can make a carefully-built life topple like a house of cards." I was never one to play the "what-if" game. I never wanted to be an old woman, looking back on her life and wondering what if?

Chapter 6

Rockport

THERE IS NEVER a good time for a funeral. But this was definitely one of the worst times.

The morning of our flight to Boston, Hubbell phoned. His grandmother had died.

I had briefly met her when I brought Hubbell homemade chicken soup because he was complaining of a cold. He had neglected to tell me his grandmother from Massachusetts had flown in for her eighty-fifth birthday. Anyway, when I paid a surprise visit with a large container of soup — still warm from the stove — he seemed pleased by my culinary thoughtfulness and eagerly showed me off to his grandma. But I was taken aback — hurt, really — by the fact that he hadn't mentioned his grandma was visiting, which should have been a big deal. Unless she was a mean old lady and he was embarrassed to have me meet her, but she didn't seem like that at all. From our brief intro, it was apparent she was surprised her grandson had a new girlfriend. Why hadn't he bragged to her about me? Not being privy to her visit and him not telling her about me was a major letdown for me in our relationship. Had I known she was visiting, I would have worn something more presentable than my grey sweats and flip-flops.

She went peacefully in her sleep. It was her long-time and loyal housekeeper who found her and put Grandma's teeth back in before making the phone call.

Hubbell took a different flight than us. He flew with his parents and headed in the opposite direction after landing in Boston. They were traveling to Marion, a suburb near Cape Cod, whereas I was journeying to the other Cape — Cape Ann, on the North Shore of Massachusetts.

Hubbell insisted I go forward with my plans, and as soon as the funeral and its aftermath concluded, he'd rent a car and drive up to us in Rockport. I never was taken in and considered "family" by Hubbell's parents, so I didn't push to attend Grandma's funeral to support Hubbell. He also convinced me that I'd had my fair share of funerals, and I deserved a long weekend away with friends, so I agreed. I went with Gloria and Cooper and tried not to feel like a third wheel. Thankfully, they didn't treat me as one.

We flew in over Boston Harbor, sparkling in the midday sun. Once we landed, Cooper told us we had to take a bus, a train, and another train until we were literally on the right tracks headed for Rockport. Cooper convinced us there was no sense in renting a car at the airport because his grandfather's old, gas-guzzling but reliable 1986 Jeep Wagoneer was parked in their garage with the keys under the seat. It sounded sweet. And even though the public transportation was tiring and endless, it was an eye-opener. Back in Texas, we didn't rely on public transport to get us around as much as it seemed Bostonians did. Everyone drove in Texas. Sure, we had the Metrorail in Houston and the TRE — Trinity Railway Express — in Fort Worth, but honestly, I may have been on it once or twice, and it was never packed like this Blue line and Purple line was. As I was trying to decipher the color-coded map, seeing that there was even a Green line and an Orange line, Cooper took my hand and gently trailed my finger along the red line, tapping at where a stop, Harvard Square, was enlarged in bold print. "And if you go to Harvard, you ride the Red line," he said mischievously.

"I can see that," I said, feeling flustered as I quickly shook my hand away before Gloria, who was fishing in her backpack for gum, saw us. "I'll ride the Metro when I'm at Rice. When I toured the campus, I was told that's how students get around town."

He only nodded, then moved closer to me when more people got on. There weren't any free seats, so we were standing and holding onto the metal pole above our heads, swaying as the train screeched along. I was impressed by how in control Cooper became. This was his territory, and he was in charge.

It seemed Gloria was getting turned on watching his protective demeanor because she was constantly grabbing at him and kissing him when the opportunity arose. She accidentally fell into him when the train took a sharp turn. As the lights flickered and the sound was piercing, iron on iron, Gloria acted as if she was a damsel in distress.

"Oh my God," she shrieked, as if this was a roller coaster ride.

He took her in, laughed at her naivety, and practically swallowed her.

I was completely jealous and felt ashamed. I looked away, gazing out of the large window, trying to picture myself flirting with Hubbell.

* * *

Cooper gave us the nickel tour of his grandparents' enchanting cottage. It was bigger on the inside than it looked on the outside. Surprisingly, it wasn't cluttered like most grandparents' homes can be. In my opinion, I think not wanting to part with things even if they aren't of use any longer has something to do with growing up during The Great Depression. This obviously wasn't the case with them. It did contain a lot of stuff, but it was neatly placed and organized. An entire wall had built-in shelves with lights, and I imagined each item on them held a story.

There was no food in the house, so our immediate hunger was satiated by a cheeseburger at the local hot spot. Cooper promised he'd go food shopping later. The three of us were gung-ho for being beach bums during the day, even though the water was far too cold to swim in, and then hanging home at night playing cards and drinking. Cooper and Gloria knew how to play poker and insisted on teaching me. I was good at Rummy 500 and preferred we play that, but they tried to convince me that it would be fun to play strip poker when Hubbell arrived. Anything involving the word 'strip' seriously needed tequila, and I didn't want a repeat of what happened to Gloria and me at the wedding. Bud Light was sufficient enough for me, and staying clothed!

My room was once the attic, and from the one window, I could see the sun glistening on the waves of the green Atlantic Ocean. The full-sized brass bed was draped with what looked like a vintage handmade quilt, with two nightstands on either side that held tiny lamps made to look like old-fashioned lanterns. It was very romantic, and I couldn't wait to share it with Hubbell.

As I stood looking out the window, I thought about Mom. She would have loved Rockport. The many art studios and small shops along the winding Main Street looked inviting, and I couldn't wait to get started exploring them.

We were browsing in an art gallery when a teakettle's whistle blew. I panicked and instinctively grabbed the person closest to me...Cooper!

Gloria howled, "Jeez, Dakota, you act as if you just saw a rat!"

Cooper laughed too, yet held on to me longer than I thought necessary. He said that it had startled him, too.

Ever since I was shot, I'm easily startled. Obviously, Gloria didn't get this, but Cooper did — he understood a lot.

"Sorry about that," the artist said, returning from the back. "Forgot about it."

Her loose-fitting, tie-dyed dress was so long it swept the floor. She offered, "Would you all like some chamomile tea?"

"No, thank you," the three of us said in unison as we finished browsing and were making our way single file through the narrow, framed door.

"Come again. Next time I promise I won't scare you!" the artist called.

Gloria was already out of the store and waiting for us as Cooper chuckled and replied, "Okay. Thank you." He gestured for me to exit first, allowing his hand to graze my back, sending shivers through me.

We browsed the next store — a spacious gallery with much better lighting. The walls were painted a bright white and on them hung large canvases. I admired an oil painting of waves breaking on a raw, sunless day — no people in sight, but it made me feel like I was there — out of the painter's view. I could feel the ocean's strength and the water's bitter chill. It was powerful, warning me away. Yet daring me to plunge right in.

Gloria stopped and stood beside me.

"Boring," she stated and took to the one that depicted a beach day on the Fourth of July.

"Too busy," I commented, "especially all the red, white, and blue swimsuits, towels, beach balls, and Frisbees." I pointed, being careful not to touch the canvas. "And look, even someone's boogie board has the American flag on it! Obviously, the artist is depicting Independence Day — but in my opinion, his over-the-top embellishment ruins it."

Gloria looked closer at the small label on the wall next to the painting and read the title aloud, "The Fourth of July," and in a teacher kind of way, she said, "Very observant, Miss Dakota!"

"That's when you met Hubbell, right?" Cooper chimed in from behind.

I was surprised Cooper knew how Hubbell and I met, 'cause I'd never told him. He'd obviously asked Gloria or Hubbell when I wasn't present.

"Yeah," I finally answered. "We met at Mr. Trenton's annual decked out, Independence Day bash." I smiled at the memory; *Trenton's Bash* embroidered on Hubbell's polo. I admired the short sleeves tight around his biceps as he handed me a frothy, cold beer and served a few others theirs before he had another bartender cover for him as he led me away, holding my hand in a tender but firm grasp. I'd only known him for a minute, but there was immediate chemistry between us. I inwardly reminisced about our make-out session while staring at another painting. God, how I wished he were with me right now.

"Let's get some ice cream," Gloria cheerily suggested.

"Yeah, I could go for strawberry ice cream," Cooper agreed but winked at me.

That day when my car broke down and Cooper had come to my rescue, driving me to my old home, he had admired a photograph of me as a young child, licking around a dripping ice cream. He had asked if I remembered the flavor since it was a black and white photo. I did — it was strawberry. So, this was kind of our inside joke. I was thankful Gloria hadn't seen his wink or the smile I shot back — she was looking in the window of a jewelry store where necklaces were draped over a piece of driftwood.

Gloria knew right away she wanted a double-scoop chocolate chip cone and ordered first, leaving Cooper and me reading the plethora of flavors handwritten on the enormous chalkboard hanging on the wall behind the counter.

"I'll be outside waiting for y'all on the bench," Gloria called, plucking a few paper napkins from the dispenser and heading out the door.

I wanted to try their black cherry chocolate chip for a change instead of my usual strawberry, but Cooper stuck with strawberry and sweetly offered to trade if I had buyer's remorse.

Even though Cooper and I had ordered the same size, the server scooped more for me. It was cute how Cooper compared his cone to mine with a pout, then playfully whispered loud for the scooper to hear, "Because you look so good in those cut-offs."

Scooper-boy raised his brows and enthusiastically nodded.

Cooper laughed. "See? I told ya!"

I just rolled my eyes.

I let Cooper take my seat on the bench next to Gloria when Hubbell texted me. I wanted to read it away from them. I couldn't help but feel hurt over him texting instead of calling. But once I read it, I understood — he was still in church.

im staring @ virgin mary. thinkin of u.

I let out a laugh.

need to stay another day.

His news knocked the wind out of me.

I texted back: *What*?

priest giving special mass for g. im srry. gtg

I texted: *K. Luv u.* and waited

But nothing. *No luv u 2.*

I slipped my cell back in my shorts pocket, disappointed.

"Is something wrong?" Cooper asked as he and Gloria approached me.

"No," I lied.

"Sooo?" Gloria asked, "any news with Hubbell's ETA?"

I shrugged my shoulders, gave a clueless look, and walked ahead of Gloria and Cooper, pretending to be interested in the shops. I recalled the first time I had heard the ETA acronym.

It was when my car broke down on the interstate, and I had waited with Cooper for the tow truck to arrive. Of course, I had called Luke to let him know what was going on. He was so relieved Cooper was there with me and told me Triple A's ETA — he had to explain — the Estimated Time of Arrival — was an hour! Thankfully the truck appeared a lot sooner, and my mom's old car was towed away within twenty minutes. The driver gave me the creeps, and when I ignored the blatant advance he made behind Cooper's back, he assumed Cooper and I were married. I hadn't even hit legal drinking age, and the idiot had called me ma'am!

I threw my half-eaten ice cream into the nearby trash can. I had lost my appetite. If Savannah were with me, I would have given it to her. I turned around and called, "Cooper, where's there a toy store? I want to bring something back for Savannah."

As Cooper and I exited the souvenir shop with a rubber lobster for Savannah, Gloria whisked out of some fancy boutique that also carried lingerie. There were a few pieces of sexy undergarments tastefully displayed in the window.

She was swinging a fuchsia paper bag tied closed with a black ribbon, like a clock's pendulum, acting all giddy, and skipped to us. We couldn't help but smile. Then she looked into Cooper's eyes and said in a sultry voice, "Honey, wait till you see what I bought!"

Gloria was really a positive, upbeat person. I suddenly felt confused as to why Cooper wasn't crazy for her. Why didn't he love her the way he loved me? I wished I could be more like Gloria — crazy, fun, sexy, and flirtatious. And it wasn't as if she wasn't physically attractive. She had a great figure — a voluptuous chest that she regularly accented with low-cut shirts, pretty dark brown hair that bounced off her shoulders every time she threw back her head and laughed. Great smile, perfectly straight white teeth, and her nose — maybe a tad too big for her face — was spotted with just the right amount of freckles, which my mom used to refer to as angel kisses. Gloria exuded an overall confidence that was the most attractive thing about her.

As we headed back to the house, I knew Gloria would model what she had bought, and it'd lead to more. So I decided to take a bike ride.

"I eyed a few bikes in the garage during the nickel tour — would it be all right if I borrowed one?" I asked.

"Great idea. Just give us ten minutes," Cooper said.

I saw the disappointed look on Gloria's face, so I quickly acted.

"If you two don't mind, I'd like to explore on my own and find a quiet place. It was this time last year when my dad died, so I want to say a few prayers. By myself, if you don't mind," I repeated.

"Oh," he answered, somewhat miffed.

What the hell? Doesn't he want to have some alone time with his girlfriend?

"Well, let me check the tires — see which bike is safe for you to ride."

"No, that's all right. I think I can handle it."

I opened the old barn-like doors to the garage. The sunlight poured in, and I could see more clearly which one was the 'safe' bicycle to ride. From the house, I heard Gloria shriek with laughter and could only imagine what was happening. Grateful I had something to distract me for a while, I pushed the teal bicycle with a wicker basket out of the garage. As I hopped onto the bike, I was reminded how much fun bike riding is. I left the driveway and pedaled down the sloping street, and the further I went, the larger the homes became.

There were quaint signs along the way directing one to a B & B or an inn, and with it, a NO VACANCY sign hung. I turned left onto Straitsmouth Way, which had seven-foot stone pillars on either side. Every home was set back from the road, with magnificent green lawns and bushes of every kind used in the landscape. It was the end of spring, and they were all in bloom with their fragrant scents: lilacs, rhododendrons, and azaleas. I wondered who lived in these houses. Were they old? Rich? The cars told me they were or maybe just lived in debt. I could hear my dad's comment: "Can't judge a man's wealth by what he drives," and my mom's rebuttal: "You shouldn't judge a person at all by the size of their home or the car they drive but by the size of their heart." And my dad agreeing with her: "I know, honey, just as long as they're humble."

I smiled at the memory and kept rolling along. I passed an old cemetery that went back to colonial times. Time had stopped for these poor souls more than 300 years ago. I had decided to rest and read a few of the gravestones, and that's when it hit me. Tears welled up as I knelt at a grave that shared my father's name. Jethro.

* * *

Two hours later, I returned. The sky was beautiful. Purple and pink clouds formed, and the smell of the sea floated in the air. I felt at peace…until a furious Cooper bolted out and shouted as if it were past my curfew, "Where have you been?"

"Holy shit! Take it easy," I shouted back.

"Don't tell me to take it easy. You don't know this area. I thought you got lost," he explained, not letting go of his father-like demeanor.

"And abducted by aliens?" I added sarcastically as I eased myself off the bike and started walking it into the garage, trying to ignore any further accusations. The garage was dim. Only a small stream of sunlight shone in — just enough for me to see where to place the bike. As I hitched the kickstand open with my foot, I sensed Cooper right behind me. I turned. My face was very near his chest. His shirt smelled of Gloria's perfume.

"Where's Gloria?" I asked.

"In the shower," he answered in a deep breath as he pointed to the back wall of the garage. "Outdoor shower." Then he pulled me into his chest and held me as he quietly said, "You scared me, Dakota. I thought something terrible had happened to you."

"I'm sorry," I relented. He really seemed concerned with my safety.

"I just want it to be you and me, Dakota…why can't it?"

I ignored giving the obvious answer to that stupid question as I shifted against him and offered up my face. He smoothed away my hair from my neck and kissed it. His tender lips crept to my cheek, then finally to my eager lips once again. It had been months since we last kissed at my old home, but I hadn't forgotten what an insatiable kisser he was. I found myself unbuttoning his shirt as his hands reached under my shirt. Our passion was fierce, and just as suddenly as it was ignited, it was doused as if a bucket of freezing cold water was thrown on us. The shower pipes abruptly stopped, making a loud screeching sound. We both pushed away from each other. He quickly buttoned up his shirt.

Gloria hollered playfully, "Cooper, where are you? I thought you would've joined me!"

He swiftly stepped in through the kitchen's back door just as she was coming in through the slider off the back deck into the cozy family room.

Moments later, I appeared with a cheery, "Hi!"

"Oh, good. You're finally back. Cooper's been worried about you. He was about to take the car out and search for you. I told him if you weren't back by dark, I'd okay a search party, but until then, I convinced him you were a big girl and could take care of yourself!" She came in for a hug. "Was I right, girlfriend?" she teased.

I inwardly cringed. I was the worst friend ever. I was a "Frenemy" and deserved to be scalped and hanged. But I answered back playfully, "You were right!" as we hugged, and I took a whiff of her hair. "You smell great. What shampoo is that?"

Cooper was pouring himself a tall rum and coke.

"Pantene," she answered, and then she scolded, "Coop, don't drink too much. We have to meet Hubbell at Faneuil Hall in a few."

"What?" I asked.

"Oh, yeah. While you were out biking, Hubbell called. You left your cell in the bathroom. Glad I heard it. Hope you didn't mind that I answered it — only because I saw who it was."

"No. I'm glad you did. I purposely left it behind, believe it or not. I wanted to explore without any distractions."

"Unbelievable! I'd die without my phone!" Gloria cried. "But good for you, Dakota — you're one in a million."

Cooper still looked peeved. I tried not to laugh.

"What's Faneuil Hall?" I asked.

"One of Boston's historic landmarks," Cooper answered. Then with a slightly furrowed brow, he added, "Good thing you didn't fall and hurt yourself since you didn't have your cell phone."

"You mean to tell me there aren't any Good Samaritans in Rockport to help a lone injured cyclist?" I asked with sass.

He took a sip of his drink and kept the glass by his mouth while staring at me, still looking annoyed.

"Just ignore him, Dakota," said Gloria as she waved him off. "But honestly, Dakota, even I've heard of Faneuil Hall — Quincy Market," she said as she took hold of the Sam's Summer Ale Cooper passed to her. She took a swig and then pointed to the picture of Sam Adams on the bottle and said with a laugh, "Sam Adams himself gave inspirational speeches from Faneuil Hall!"

"Yeah. She's right. Faneuil Hall has been a meeting hall and marketplace since 1742," Cooper added.

"Okay. Enough with the history lesson. Can I have one?" I asked rather abruptly. They were making me feel like a child.

"A rum and coke or a beer?" Cooper asked.

"A beer," I answered. "So what does this Faneuil Hall offer now — in the twenty-first century?"

"Bars!" Gloria laughed.

"And restaurants, and shops, and an amazing food court with a range of vendors serving everything from authentic Middle-Eastern food to simple hotdogs loaded with anything your little heart desires. And outside in the courtyard, at certain times, there are performers. Usually acrobatic jugglers, magicians, musicians — you know. It's a real tourist attraction," Cooper explained.

"Sounds fun," I said.

Gloria panicked. "Wait! Dakota doesn't have a fake ID!"

"No worries. We're going to go to The Shamrock. My friend Robin, from Harvard, bartends there," Cooper said calmly.

It was nice of Cooper to come to my defense, but did he have to remind us where he went to college? It wouldn't be like me if I didn't give it right back to him. I enjoyed bantering with him, and I think he relished it just as much.

"So, with an Ivy League education, that's all he could get?" I wisecracked. "Only a bartending job?"

"Only on the weekends so she can pay for law school."

His response was just as smug as my sass.

"Oh. What type of law?" I asked, easing up. I had been defeated. I was suddenly nervous about meeting this female bartending friend and wanted her to like me.

"I forget. You can ask her when you meet her," he said, looking at his watch, "in ninety minutes. You'd better go get ready. Towels are in the closet at the top of the stairs in case you want to shower after your long bike ride."

Gloria's head was practically in the cupboards, searching as she whined, "There's nothing to eat here. I feel like something crunchy and salty. Coop, I thought you were going to go food shopping."

"I was, but you wouldn't let me go. You insisted I cuddle with you," he reminded her. "At least I made it to the liquor store. I should've picked up a bag of pretzels at checkout. Sorry. Let me go now while you two get ready. It's just down the street. I thought we'd just go for a few drinks and appetizers in Boston and then head back here for dinner. I can grill us some steaks," he said as he scooted out to the garage, and I headed upstairs to take a shower.

Chapter 7

Faneuil Hall

COOPER FOUND a parking spot on the street with an already-fed meter for the remaining hour — past eight o'clock meters are free. I figured finding a metered spot was a rarity because he acted as if he'd just won the lottery, and then not having to feed it eight quarters was an added bonus. We had passed a few parking garages on our walk to Faneuil Hall with signs that read, *$40 All Night Parking*! I realized then why he had been so darn excited — city living was expensive, even for cars.

I saw Hubbell and ran to him. He was still dressed in a suit and tie. He took me in. We kissed but not the way-too-long kind you see in the movies. We knew Cooper and Gloria were nearby, waiting for us.

"You look handsome," I said, smoothing down his silk tie and then immediately regretting I had said such a stupid thing. For God's sake, he had just come from a funeral.

He didn't acknowledge my compliment. He lightly took my hand and began to walk towards Cooper and Gloria. "I can only stay for a few drinks and dinner, and then I've got to head back."

"What?" I said, sounding both surprised and pissed off as I freed my hand from his.

"Dakota. I told you. I have to attend mass tomorrow morning. The priest is making a dedication to my grandmother."

"I thought he did that already," I said, totally confused.

"At the funeral?" he said, rolling his eyes and combing his hair with both hands, looking annoyed and disappointed that he had made the trek into the city.

There was an awkward silence among the four of us before Hubbell mumbled an insincere, "Sorry."

"No worries, dude. Tomorrow night we'll eat lobster on my grandparents' deck and take in the view," Cooper assured us, sounding totally pleased he had another night of being alone with me.

"Tomorrow? Sunday? But we're leaving Monday! That leaves you only one night with me in Rockport. Wait! You *are* planning on staying with me, right?"

"Yeah, Dakota. And I planned on my grandmother dying."

Cooper and Gloria walked briskly ahead of us.

A frantic "I'm sorry" were the only words that came to mind.

"I need a drink! I fucking paid thirty dollars to park my car!"

I was secretly pleased he hadn't found a metered spot, and Cooper had. Hubbell definitely seemed preoccupied, like something was on his mind, and I had this hunch it was not his deceased grandma.

We sat outside at some restaurant, sandwiched between tourists with cameras around their necks, intently looking at maps and brochures. And even though the sun was setting, the last of its intense glare peeked through the surrounding tall buildings and landed at the exact spot where our table was, hitting our faces. We decided to keep our shades on until the sun disappeared behind the skyscraper, which I was happy about because I felt tears beginning to well in my eyes. The waitress came by and greeted us, "Welcome to Joe's. I'm Amy. I'll be your server this evening. Can I start you off with an appetizer and drinks?"

"Can we get a pitcher of Bud Light and the Nacho Supreme to start, please?" Cooper took the liberty of ordering for all of us, and we were happy he did. There was tension between Hubbell and me, and Gloria already said she was craving something crunchy and salty back at the house. We hadn't had time to break into the bag of chips and jar of salsa Cooper had brought back from his grocery shopping.

"Sure," Amy said, and then the inevitable came, "Can I see some ID?"

"Sorry. Left mine at home," I lied, while the others offered theirs for Amy's inspection.

"Great. I'll bring out three glasses." Then, seeing my disappointment as I slumped back in my chair, Amy offered, "Can I get you a virgin piña colada? The bartender makes 'em awesome."

She seemed sweet. I wasn't upset with her. She was just doing her job. Besides, I knew the manager would question her if she hadn't carded us. After all, we were wearing sunglasses, looking like conspicuous idiots — especially Hubbell.

"I'll take a Pepsi, please," I said, and then suggested as Amy walked away, "Cooper, I can be the designated driver since I'm not drinking. Y'all can drink up if you want. I don't care." And I actually meant it. I didn't really care to party hardy in the famous Faneuil Hall. My mood had been deflated by the fact that Hubbell had to drive back to Marion and stay in his deceased grandmother's condo — with his parents and without me. My initial feeling of being left out returned. I was still hurt by not being asked to attend the service. So what if I wasn't Catholic? We still believed in the same God.

"I wouldn't let her unless you want to get lost," Hubbell commented. "Dakota can't find her way out of a shoebox."

Cooper immediately came to my defense. "She did all right on her bike ride today. Found her way home without any problem."

"Yeah, but you were worried." Gloria chimed in with a laugh and then gave my shoulders a quick, tight squeeze as she innocently teased, "My Cooper just loves you so much!"

Yep, he does — more than you know, was what I wanted to say, but instead, I shook my head and sputtered with my arms crossed, leaning back in my seat with my Ray-Bans still on even though the sun had disappeared. "You're a jerk, Hubbell."

No one spoke.

I was so pissed. I hated how Hubbell berated me. He was dead wrong if he thought making fun of my driving was cute, like how Gloria was lovingly teasing me. There was no comparison between the two — it didn't even come close.

Hubbell slowly took off his sunglasses and gave me a cross look but said nothing, and neither did Cooper or Gloria. They nervously looked at one another and then studied their surroundings.

Hubbell carefully folded his precious, expensive, designer sunglasses and placed them in his inside breast pocket. His eyes turned to me as he calmly replied, "You know, Dakota, I didn't expect this from you. I thought you'd understand, considering..."

"Considering what, Hubbell?" I had a hunch where he was going with it.

"Never mind." He reached for his menu, but I pushed it away.

"No! Not never mind. Yeah, I'm the expert on death. Buried both my parents."

"Yeah. That's right. So I thought you'd be a little more sympathetic towards me," he said angrily, and then added, "I fucking just buried my grandmother this morning, Dakota. Show some compassion!"

"The grandmother I accidentally met. You didn't even tell me she was visiting!"

"That's why you're pissed?" he asked, not relenting on his harsh tone.

"Maybe. And maybe I'm hurt you didn't want me to attend her funeral. To be with you, to give you support during this emotional time since I'm the expert on funerals. And now you're headed back for Sunday service, and you don't have the decency to ask if I'd like to come with you for this honorary mass the priest is giving. It's the least you could do to make me feel like part of your family. And quite honestly, Hubbell, I'm beginning to feel you're embarrassed to introduce me to your relatives."

"I thought you couldn't handle it. I know you've been through a lot."

"Really, Hubbell? Or did your parents think it best I wasn't there —
wanted their baby boy all to themselves — just like Jamaica?"

Gloria and Cooper remained quiet. Looking at each other, giving a
'what-should-we-do?' look. Gloria picked up her menu upside down and
pretended to read it. Cooper followed, but he was smart enough to hold it
right side up.

"Are you fucking kidding me? You're still upset you couldn't come to
Jamaica?"

"I'm pissed about a lot of things, Hubbell!" I exclaimed.

"Yeah? Like med school? You're pissed because I want to be a doctor?"

I didn't say anything. It was selfish of me not to be happy he got in.

"You know, Dakota, there are a lot of girls who would die for a
boyfriend who's attending Yale Medical School," he finished slowly and
arrogantly, sounding like a cocky son-of-a-bitch.

"I'm sure there are a ton, Hubbell, all lined up. Go pick yourself one.
I'm through!" I shouted and abruptly fled from my seat.

"What the fuck?" Gloria cried

"Holy shit!" Cooper said. "Didn't see that one coming." Then he told
Hubbell, "Go after her."

"No. Let her be. She'll come back," Hubbell said. Just then, Amy arrived
with the enormous platter of nachos — the guacamole, sour cream, and
salsa slowly dripping down from the heat of the melting cheese.

"Maybe I should?" Gloria suggested.

"Be my guest," Hubbell said.

"Yeah. You should," Cooper said urgently. "Or I will. I know the area
better. She could get lost."

"Okay," Gloria said, sounding relieved. "You go, honey, since you
know the area better than us."

Hubbell tucked into the nachos and didn't look up.

Chapter 8

The Ally

SURPRISINGLY, COOPER found me. I was sitting on a bench, watching a mime climb into his imaginary box. The stranger sitting next to me got up, and Cooper swiftly sat down before anyone else could. The place was packed, it being a Saturday night and Memorial Day weekend. Cooper didn't say anything to me. My eyes remained focused on the mime straight ahead of me, who was now pretending he was trapped in the box. Cooper waited for me to apologize. But I didn't turn to him when I said I was sorry.

"For what?"

"For ruining your fun weekend away."

"You didn't ruin it," he said, and then after a five-second pause, he added, "Grandma did."

I knew he was joking. Cooper was funny, and he never tried hard like Hubbell did. It just came naturally to him. I let out a laugh, which made him laugh, too.

I answered back sarcastically, "I know. Right? Grandma shouldn't have died. It's all her fault." Then I added to make up for my facetiousness, "The one time I met her, she seemed like a sweet old lady."

Cooper remained still and listened sympathetically to what I wanted to get off my chest.

"She asked me if I had any hobbies. I told her I liked to write, so she asked to hear a story of mine. I explained that they were written in a notebook, which was back at my house, but she insisted I tell her one. After

I did, she patted my head, calling it 'beautiful,' and reminded me that every good writer has something memorized. As soon as I nodded in agreement, Hubbell excused himself, offering to bring back drinks and a snack as I sat on the floor beside her chair and recited a poem I had written about my mom. Hubbell had impeccable timing, returning when I was through. His grandma took a tissue she had stuffed up her sleeve and wiped her eyes, telling me I had a gift. Honestly, Cooper, I would have liked to have said goodbye to her."

"You still can. You can always pray regardless of where you are, Dakota." Then his tone became more matter-of-fact. "And Hubbell should have wanted you with him at her funeral for support — different than what his parents can give." We still weren't looking at one another but straight ahead at the show. For a moment, I felt like Julia Roberts in *The Pelican Brief*, trying to act inconspicuously as I disclosed top secrets to Denzel Washington.

"Will you want Gloria with you?" I asked, adding, "At your grandpa's funeral?" knowing his grandfather was dying from cancer. That was why Cooper had been driving to Dallas when my car broke down on the interstate. He didn't know how serious his grandfather's illness was at the time. No one knew then of the grim prognosis.

"No. I want you," he said, turning to me and putting his hand on my thigh. He lightly kneaded it as he repeated, "I want you with me when my grandfather dies. Dakota, I want you with me... always."

I remained speechless. It was now dark, and the quaint, old-fashioned gas street lights automatically came on in succession, as if someone had just flipped the switch. Faneuil Hall looked beautiful — illuminated and very charming. I didn't know what to say, but I had the sudden urge to kiss him. I laid a soft kiss on his tender lips. He closed his eyes. My mouth moved to his ear as I whispered into it the three words he had said to me back in Fort Worth before leaving me alone: "I love you."

Cooper suddenly stood and took my hand in a lovingly firm grasp as he led us through the tourists. He threw a ten-dollar bill into the mime's derby hat, which rested on the outside of the imaginary box. The mime smiled and waved to us and then touched his heart to show his gratitude.

The architecture of Faneuil Hall was composed of short alleys in between buildings of shops and restaurants. We had walked through one from the street where we had parked, and I admired the old-world charm of it — European-looking and very romantic. Cooper led me into an empty alley and stopped. He stood over me. Pressed me with the length of his body, hard against the cold, stone wall, but immediately warmed me with his body heat. He said softly, "I never gave up thinking about our drive — our time in your old home, Dakota. It was special to me. You're so special to me, Dakota."

He liked saying my name, and I liked hearing him say it. I also thought about our drive together when we reminisced about our childhoods and our parents. When we weren't sharing our happy memories, we listened to The Rolling Stones. Then there was the way he stayed with me until I awoke after I had fainted, barely missing the coffee table. Cooper had carried me over to the sofa and covered me with my mom's afghan. The sights and smells of my home had brought a sea of memories to my subconscious, causing me to faint. I thought I could have handled returning to my old home, but apparently not, and I was glad Cooper had come in to use the bathroom. He browsed around and took a liking to the array of photos my mom had hung in the hallway between the bathroom and my and my parent's bedrooms. We flirted, and our affection for one another led to kissing — long, passionate kissing. But then I came to my senses and insisted he leave and go to his grandparents as planned. I assured him I would be all right. It was hours later that Jake Jennings appeared and who knows what would have happened if Cooper had stayed and spent the night? Maybe I wouldn't have been shot. Maybe Cooper would have wrestled with Jennings. Who knows? I touched his cheek. "I never stopped thinking about you, Cooper — although I tried."

He smiled and let out a long, quiet breath.

Instinctively I shifted against him, offering up my face.

He tenderly smoothed my lips with his thumb and said, "Not here —
too many people." And just as he finished, a group of partygoers howled
through, already hammered. "Let's head back. Gloria must be worried."

He led the way, but this time he didn't hold my hand. We had to
pretend, for Gloria's sake, that there was nothing between us. We couldn't
give two shits about Hubbell.

When we reached Joe's, Gloria was sitting alone.

"Where's Hubbell?" Cooper asked.

"He left," Gloria said. "What'd you expect?"

Now she sounded as upset as I had initially.

"I'm sorry, Gloria," I said. Inwardly I wanted to scream and be done
with it; *I'm sorry I fell in love with your boyfriend — I couldn't help it*!

"I'm sorry, too, honey," Cooper said as he bent to kiss her. She perked
up a little and said, "Let's pay the check and head back."

"Let's have one last drink at The Shamrock — I promised my friend. If
that's alright with you?"

Cooper knew better to rephrase it, asking for Gloria's permission. After
all, who knows how long Gloria was sitting alone with a pitcher of beer and
a platter of nachos? Passersby must have thought she was a weirdo.

"Sure. As long as Dakota does a shot with me!" she said as she took out
her makeup compact and started freshening up her face, looking in its tiny
mirror and dabbing her slightly shiny nose with powder.

"Sure. Why not," I answered, and then looked at Cooper and declared,
"You're driving, after all, cowboy!"

He gave a huge smile and answered, "It'd be my pleasure. As long as
you girls are happy, I'm happy!"

Chapter 9

The Shamrock

THE LINE to get in snaked all the way around the corner of the building for another ten yards. "Not waiting," Gloria firmly stated, both hands on her hips.

"Don't fret, baby doll." Cooper scrolled through his cell and then put it to his ear. His friend must have answered in a wise-ass but upbeat mood because Cooper immediately chuckled and returned, "Yep, we're fucking here — right outside!" She gave him instructions on how to skirt the line because he said with assurance as he returned his cell to his breast pocket, "Follow me." It was such a turn-on when he took control at just the right times.

He led us around to the back. We stepped over a linked chain around a set of open bulkhead doors, where a kitchen staffer in a disgustingly bloody apron was sitting on a milk crate smoking. "Hey man," he said, looking up at Cooper as if we girls were invisible. "What's up?" he asked before taking another drag of his cigarette.

"We're here for Robin," Cooper answered with a nod as we steadily made our way down the steep metal steps. I reluctantly held onto the sticky railing. Once inside, we walked across a smelly damp cement floor and past a line of kegs. We made our way up another set of wooden stairs — not as steep — and into a noisy kitchen. We were immediately overwhelmed by the smell of greasy fried food. We pushed our way through the kitchen door, and nobody stopped us. The cooks were slammed with orders, and nobody was paying us any attention.

Suddenly, "Cooper. My Cooper!" was being screamed by a very bubbly female. Seconds later, this female appeared, an enormous smile on her flawless face. She immediately took Cooper's head in her manicured hands and brought him in for a big kiss on the lips. But just as quickly as she did, she let go. She then turned to me and announced, "You must be Gloria!" Before I could correct her, she added, "You're right, Coop — she's gorgeous!"

Suddenly, Gloria pushed her way through with just as big of a smile and corrected, "No. I'm Gloria. She's Dakota."

"Of course — the prettier one!" She hugged Gloria but winked at me behind Gloria's back. Robin intuitively knew not to make Gloria jealous. And she didn't give Gloria a chance to misinterpret her flirting with Cooper. She and Gloria immediately bonded. They had the same flamboyant personality.

Cooper laughed, "See, I told you you'd love her!" He gestured to Gloria. I'm guessing Gloria was just as curious to meet this female friend of Cooper's as I was. Suddenly her name was being screamed. "Robin, get your butt over here. Your drink orders are piling up!" A guy in his mid-forties was standing at the bar, pouring beer into multiple tall glasses. I immediately apologized for all of us and told her, "Go!"

"Yep, go! Don't want to get you fired," Gloria added.

Robin reacted nonchalantly. "He'd never fire me — who'd give him blow jobs?" And with that, she walked towards the packed bar.

We followed her. "Did she just say what I think she said?" I asked Gloria as I trailed right behind her.

She laughed.

The Joker by the Steve Miller Band was playing — one of Luke's favorite songs. Robin went behind the bar and poured us three shots before she took care of her backed-up orders. "Sex on the beach!" Robin yelled

"What?" I exclaimed.

Both Cooper and Gloria laughed at my naïveté.

"The shot. It's the name of the shot!" Cooper answered, smiling at me.

I took the shot glass Cooper was handing me and thought, what the heck, and toasted, "To blowjobs and sex on the beach!"

My friends laughed, and a half-dozen college-age guys overheard me and repeated my toast before they knocked back their shots. One stared at me, smiled, and gestured for me to come over, but Cooper derailed it by taking hold of my shoulders and gently turning me towards Robin. "Make Dakota your specialty."

Chapter 10

Car Ride

GLORIA WAS LAUGHING and teasing, calling me a "lightweight" as she buckled me in. Then she kissed me on the tip of my nose and said, "Goodnight," before climbing into the front passenger seat beside Cooper.

"She'll be fine once she gets some food in her. Won't be long 'til I get the steaks on the grill."

I thought it was cute that Cooper wanted to make sure I ate. I let the car ride lull me, but we weren't even out of the city before Gloria murmured in a hushed tone, "Hubbell left for the Omni."

"What? As in the Omni Hotel?" Cooper asked, puzzled.

"Yep, the one around the corner from Faneuil Hall — that's what he said."

"Why?"

"His old girlfriend, Laura, is staying there."

"What?" Cooper sounded pissed.

I wanted to shout the same question but pretended to be zonked so Gloria would divulge more.

"Yeah. Laura showed up at Grandma's funeral. Then she told Hubbell she was headed into town for the night in case he wanted to join her."

My mind was racing. I was fuming mad. I wanted to scream. I suddenly felt sober, but I remained silent with my eyes still closed.

"That son of a bitch. So he really didn't have to return to Marion and attend mass for his grandma?" Cooper asked angrily.

"No. He wasn't lying about that. Old girlfriend was planning on going to that, too, but wanted to stay in the city — not some motel in the boonies. Can't blame her. Supposedly, she drove from Connecticut. And they went out for five years."

"Five years!" Gloria repeated, aghast.

"How do you know all this?" Cooper asked, and I thought the same. Geez, we weren't gone for that long. How come Hubbell divulged all this to my best friend? She had found out that he was accepted into Yale Medical School before I did, and now she knew about this girlfriend of five years. He never told me about her. How come? Had this girl ripped his heart out so badly he couldn't even mention her?

Gloria defended him, "He was pissed, Cooper. He was pissed Dakota publicly broke up with him. He was pissed that you scampered after her like she was a lost puppy. I thought it was sweet of you and only wished Hubbell had thought of it. After all, Dakota's his girlfriend — not yours. Anyway, when Amy came to see how our nachos were, he ordered himself two shots of tequila. When they came, he downed them both quickly and confessed he was still in love with Laura. He went on to say he hadn't realized it until she appeared in church for his grandmother's funeral, looking gorgeous. That's a quote. Supposedly Laura loved Grandma as if she were her own grandmother — or so she said. That's what he said."

"Holy shit! Was he planning on breaking up with Dakota tonight?" he asked.

"I don't know. He didn't say. Doesn't matter now — Dakota beat him to it."

"I'm glad Dakota's passed out. Don't tell her, okay? She doesn't need to know just yet. She has been through a lot already," Cooper insisted.

"All right, fine with me. I hate to be the bearer of bad news anyway." Changing the subject, Gloria asked, "Does this car have anything else other than Glenn Miller cassettes?"

I could hear her shuffling them. "Oh, Barbra Streisand. Dakota's mom loved her." She must have come across the soundtrack for *The Way We*

Were' cause she said, "Can you believe Hubbell's mom named him Hubbell after seeing this movie? I think Streisand's pretty awesome, too, but I don't think I'd name my son Hubbell."

"Yentl, then," Cooper joked.

Gloria laughed. "Very funny."

I nearly busted out a laugh, too.

"Pretty impressive, baby, that you know Yentl."

"I may have watched the movie once or twice with Grandma," Cooper shared.

Gloria put the cassettes back and fiddled with the radio. Cooper stopped her at a song. It was The Rolling Stones', *Paint It Black.* I smiled. I happily recalled listening to another Rolling Stones favorite when he drove me to Fort Worth after my car broke down.

As soon as we neared the house, my phone went off. I pretended it woke me up. How could I have fallen into a deep sleep after all that had happened? I read who it was. I answered with immediate concern. "Luke, is everything all right?"

"Geez, does something have to be wrong for me to call?"

I laughed. "No, but it's late."

"Well, I was thinking of you, and I knew you'd be up. I just wanted to call to tell you I love you and miss you."

Then I heard Savannah bellowing in the background, "Tell her, Daddy! Tell her!" … and a dog barking.

"Luke, did you get another dog?" I asked excitedly, a tad disappointed they did it without including me.

"No!" he cried. "Of course we didn't — not without you!"

I sighed in relief.

"We're just dog sitting for a friend," he explained.

"What kind is it?"

"A basset hound. You know, the dogs with droopy eyes."

"What's its name?"

"Pooh Bear," Savannah giggled into the phone.

"Hi, Savannah. I miss you. Are you and Pooh Bear going to sleep together?"

"I don't know." Then I heard her ask, "Dad, can me and Pooh Bear sleep together?"

"All right. Just as long as you think he and Paddington Bear will get along," Luke answered.

Hearing Savannah's adorable voice and infectious giggle were exactly what I needed at the moment. I smiled and asked, "How's Mrs. Prego?"

"Amber Lee's awesome. She's asleep, or else she'd be on the phone asking you, 'How's Hubbell?'"

I ignored that last part and asked, "Isn't it way past Savannah's bedtime?"

"Yes, but she wanted to go with me to get the dog, and she took a nap today."

"You're such a softy."

"I can't help it. "Then I heard him holler, "No, not in the house! Outside!"

I laughed.

"I've gotta go, Dakota. The dog just peed on the kitchen floor. Love you."

"Love you, too."

Immediately Gloria asked, "Is everything all right?"

"Yeah, Luke was just checking in."

"Good," Cooper responded as he pulled into the driveway. "How are you feeling, Dakota?"

"Starving."

He smiled. "I'll start dinner right away. Bought steak."

"Yum," Gloria said. "I'm starving, too."

* * *

I sat down, served myself some salad, and drizzled it with bleu cheese dressing as Cooper served me a nice-looking T-bone.

After I savored the first bite, I complimented, "This is so delicious, Cooper."

"Thank the cow," Cooper said. "I just grilled it."

"Yeah, but the marinade is awesome," I enthused.

"Just a little salt and pepper," Cooper said humbly.

"Really? That's all?" Gloria teased, acting suspicious in a cutesy manner. "I could have sworn I saw a dish of some gooey stuff."

"All right, maybe I brushed a little something on them, but it's a family secret, and if I tell you…" He bent closer to her and playfully threatened in a loud whisper, "I'm going to have to kill you."

"Impossible. Dakota and I can take you out!"

"I would love that," he admitted, grinning.

I chimed in, "Hello? Do I have any say in this matter? Didn't mean for my complimenting the chef to lead to a threesome or murder."

They both laughed and said simultaneously, "You are so adorable, Dakota."

I was feeling so much better by the end of supper. Cooper was right; I needed something to eat. I was surprised at how at ease I was with my break-up with Hubbell, but honestly, it had been building up for a while. I think deep down, I knew the day would come. It may have been sooner than I expected, but I was fine with it. And I was really happy I was. I think I was relieved I didn't break his heart. He was headed to a hotel in Boston to meet his old girlfriend, go up to her room and make love. From what I've heard, hotel sex was the best. Why was that? Because you can make a mess and not have to clean it up? Or you feel uninhibited — not caring if your neighbors hear you because you'll never see them again? I offered to clean up the dinner dishes, but Gloria and Cooper insisted I go on up to bed.

"I'm fine, really. You pulled dinner together. Let me at least clean up."
I tried to persuade them, but they wouldn't hear of it, so I did as I was told.
I headed up to my room as if I was a child, and it was past my bedtime. I
decided to take another shower before climbing into bed in the room I was
supposed to share with Hubbell.

It was past midnight, and I was too exhausted to read. Before turning
off the light, I lay back, feeling the cool sea breeze flutter in the tiny open
window — making the linen curtains dance. I took in the coziness of the
room and admired how Cooper's grandmother had decorated it. A wooden
sign above the doorway read *A Home By The Sea Is A Little Slice Of Heaven*.
On the dresser sat a teddy bear wearing a Navy uniform, and in the corner
was a basket filled with wooden puzzles and books. They weren't only
weathered but looked vintage — probably her daughter's when she was a
child, then passed along to Cooper and TJ. And now they belonged to her
great-grandchildren — TJ's kids, Summer and Charlie. I smiled at the
thought and remembered how Cooper thought it was so cool when he
found out my middle name was Summer. I turned off the lamp on my
nightstand and pulled the quilt to my chin. The full moon cascaded
perfectly over the word *Heaven* and I smiled, thinking it was a sign from
my parents. Before I closed my eyes, the door slowly opened. Somebody
had come in. For a split second, it was eerie, but then I recognized the faint
smell of Cooper's cologne.

He leaned over me and brushed his lips gently against mine. Then he
said softly, "Sweet dreams, Dakota," and then he was gone. The door closed
gently behind him.

What the heck. Who was I kidding? I was so calm about my breakup
with Hubbell and his rendezvous with 'Connecticut girl' because I loved
Cooper, and Cooper loved me. Breakups were way easier when there was
someone else waiting in the wings. I prayed Gloria would find someone
else in college and initiate the breakup with Cooper. It would be better that
way, and no one would get hurt.

Chapter 11

The Morning After

I AWOKE to the smell of freshly brewed coffee. I sauntered into the kitchen, poured myself a cup, and made my way to the back deck where Gloria was basking in the morning sun wearing a skimpy nightie. "Good morning, my darling Dakota," she said in a drawn-out Southern-belle type voice.

I laughed, "Good morning, Miss Scarlet. Are you trying out for the lead in *Gone With the Wind*?"

"Frankly, my dear, I am nursing a hangover, and I don't give a damn," she answered, changing her voice — impersonating Clark Gable perfectly. She really was good at acting. I was sorry I missed her last play at school — the musical *Fiddler On The Roof*, where she played the matchmaker. How ironic.

I asked, "Where's Cooper?"

"Said he had to do something. He'll be back soon," she answered, not in the least bit curious as to what it was he had to do. I, on the other hand, was curious. Then, just at that moment, before my mind raced to all sorts of weird thoughts, like he was at the Omni, pulverizing Hubbell, Cooper appeared.

"Good morning, girls," he greeted us, and he bent down and kissed Gloria's forehead. There were no packages in his hands, so he didn't go shopping, but then he said, "I bought some apple strudel from a bakery on Bearskin Neck. The people who own it are from Austria."

"Do they wear lederhosen?" Gloria teased.

"No, but the frau does do her hair up in that native braid," he answered while curling his own hair with his fingers as if playing charades.

We laughed.

"Help yourself. It's on the kitchen counter. I already had too much."

* * *

We spent the entire day on the beach, relaxing. Sometimes my mind wandered — did Hubbell spend the morning in bed with 'Connecticut girl?' Did they even make it to church for Grandma's mass? Was she having brunch with his family, clinking champagne glasses filled with mimosas? Toasting Grandma's life with snotty Dr. and Mrs. Cavanaugh? I had to remind myself not to care.

"I'm going to swim out to that raft," I announced as I got up from the blanket the three of us shared, thankful they hadn't made me feel like a third wheel.

Cooper lifted his head, leaning back on his elbows. He asserted, "No. It's too dangerous."

I guffawed, "Who are you, my father? It can't be too dangerous, or else they wouldn't have it there. And besides, I saw a group of kids swimming to it." I pointed, "See, they're out on it now!" I said, rolling my eyes at him.

"Let's go with her," Cooper suggested to Gloria.

"No way! You go. The water is freezing. The only way you'll get me in that water is by carrying me," she said, not moving or opening her eyes. "But you wouldn't be that stupid," she warned.

I could tell Cooper was psyched that she'd suggested he go. She was completely clueless about Cooper's feelings for me. Hadn't she noticed how he always defended me? Or did she believe our BFF status would never be jeopardized by a boy? I should be happy she was utterly oblivious to his continuous flirting with me.

He rolled over and kissed her flat, getting-tanned, belly.

"Go! You're blocking my sun," she scolded, lightly tossing his head.

Cooper and I headed together into the frigid water to swim to the raft. I wondered if he was hoping as much as I was that the kids on it would leave by the time we got out there so we could be alone. I wanted to tell him I wasn't really in a drunken stupor the night before and that I'd heard everything Gloria had said about Hubbell and his old girlfriend, Laura.

Even though we didn't challenge each other, "Race you to it!" I acted as if we had. I was the first to climb the short ladder and leaned down to him. He was still in the water, and I playfully announced, "I won!"

He smiled, took hold of the ladder, and made his way up onto the raft.

My little wish came true. The kids all decided to do cannonballs as soon as we boarded. We were all alone.

I lay down. And Cooper laid on top of me!

"Are you crazy? Gloria may see!" I hollered, pushing him off of me.

"Through the binoculars she doesn't have?" he asked as he acquiesced and rolled over next to me, taking hold of my hand.

I shook that away, too. "What if she borrows someone's? You know, to see if we made it all safe and sound."

"She doesn't care," he said.

"Whatever. I just don't want her to get hurt. One breakup this weekend is enough," I reminded him.

"Yeah, you're taking it pretty well. I know it was you who broke up with him, but still."

I blurted out, "Cooper, I know about Laura."

"What? For how long?"

"Just last night, when y'all found out. I didn't even know he was in a five-year relationship before me."

"I thought you were passed out."

"Nope. I was emotionally drained over what had happened — breaking up with Hubbell the day of his grandma's funeral. That was really mean of me. He was right; I wasn't showing empathy for his feelings. I felt like shit, but he didn't come after me when I thought he should have. But then you showed up, sitting next to me, and made me feel like it wasn't my fault. That nothing is ever my fault. You're always there for me, Cooper. Unexpectedly. You appear just when I need you the most."

He didn't utter a word.

I sighed and continued, "You showed up at the hospital the night of my uncle's car accident to see how he was and if I was alright. Of course, I wasn't. I couldn't bear to lose my uncle too. Hadn't God taken enough from me? First my mother, then my father. The one-year mark of his passing is coming up."

"I remember. That's why you wanted to be alone on your bike ride... to find a quiet place to pray."

I nodded. It was partly true. The other side of it was that I had a hunch Gloria wanted some alone time with Cooper.

"Where did you end up — for this *solitude?*"

"Believe it or not, a cemetery. I find them very peaceful. And I'm not afraid to walk through one at night like some people are. I actually came across a very old gravestone marked 'Jethro.' That was my dad's name."

"I remember," Cooper said. "Your uncle mentioned him in his speech at the wedding."

I smiled. Impressed with Cooper's memory. Was he always this good, or did he make a special effort to remember things that were important in my life... because he loved me?

"Anyway, there was my uncle, in critical condition — waiting for his rare blood type the hospital didn't have enough of, and YOU have it. You donated blood for his operation, for God's sake!"

Cooper remained quiet.

I finally had the courage to say what I had been feeling for some time but was too afraid he might think it weird of me. At this point, there was nothing to lose. "Geez, Cooper. Is it a sign that we should be together?"

Nothing, not even a "hmmm," slipped out of his mouth. What the fuck? Had he gone deaf? I continued, "I believe it's a sign, so that's why I kissed you and told you I loved you last night. But then I thought, what did I do? Cooper's my best friend's boyfriend, and I am the worst friend ever, so now I'm sort of afraid I'll have bad karma."

Cooper still hadn't responded. I realized I had been madly rambling on, sounding crazy. Cooper probably was rolling his eyes — mine were closed to the sun. Then it hit me. I'd relate how I was feeling to a movie. That's what Mom always did with Dad. She swore that more truth comes out of jest.

"I feel like…like Sister Maria. Should I become a nun or leave the abbey for Captain von Trapp?"

Cooper chuckled, "*The Sound of Music* is one of my favorite movies."

I was relieved he knew it, but who didn't?

"I hope you decide to leave the abbey, as I think you'd get bored — although you'd look adorable wearing a habit."

I was grateful he found my analogy funny and didn't jump off the raft and swim back. I returned the playfulness. "Yeah? But I could be naked under it, and no one would ever suspect."

"But now I would know. My church attendance would skyrocket just to sneak a peek, and I'm not even Catholic."

I laughed and confessed, "Me neither."

"You couldn't mother my seven children if you became a nun," he said.

I smiled, feeling tickled pink. Someday, Cooper wanted to marry me. But then I remembered Hubbell had acted this way, too, on Valentine's Day, calling me 'Mrs. Cavanaugh.' So I decided not to take this too seriously, remembering my dad's words of wisdom: Take one day at a time.

I joked, keeping *The Sound of Music* theme going, "Could we name our first son Kurt? I love that name."

"Only if we can name our first daughter Gretel," he retorted. "I love that name."

And I wondered, did he really like the name, or was he just playing along? I answered anyway. "Deal." And just when it rolled from my tongue, our lips met as we both murmured, "I love you."

"And yes, Dakota," he whispered, "it is a sign. I believe in them, too."

We sealed it with a kiss and laid there for a while, basking in the sun. I hoped he was having the same thoughts I was.

Chapter 12

Hubbell Phones

THREE days after I returned from Boston, Hubbell phoned me. He had stayed on longer with his mom, helping her pack up Grandma's things. Her condo was going on the market as soon as the place "showed nicely" — getting rid of the too many framed family photographs and other personal trinkets most grandparents proudly display. It wouldn't be a grandparent's home if clutter didn't exist, especially pictures, cards, and little knick-knacks. I remembered giving my grandma a tiny pillow — the size of a traveler's clock — with a ribbon loop so it could be hung, and the endearing words, *World's Greatest Grandma*, embroidered on it. She told me it dangled from a cabinet knob in her kitchen above the coffeemaker we had given her one birthday. I remembered when visiting my dad's mom in Corpus Christi at Easter, she still had cards from Christmas taped to the fridge and told us she couldn't part with them — they were so dear to her. I wondered if Hubbell's grandma was as sentimental. I would never know.

Immediately, Hubbell confessed about his old girlfriend, Laura. I wasn't sure if he felt guilty about having sex with her the night of his grandma's funeral and wanted to get it off his chest or if he wanted to get a rise out of me since I had publicly humiliated him. Honestly, I didn't care. I allowed this information to penetrate the silence, unable to speak as I thought of Laura, wondering what she was like and if she were the type of person I'd befriend. He sounded surprised I was so calm.

"Did your friends tell you how irrational you acted?"

"No. I overheard Gloria and Cooper talking. They thought I was asleep."

"You got drunk."

I didn't respond.

"It only takes one drink, and you're done!" He laughed as if he'd just given the punch- line to a joke.

"Where did I go wrong?"

He remained silent.

"Why do you constantly belittle me?"

"Don't be so sensitive, Dakota. I'm just teasing."

Gloria teased me, but in a playful and lighthearted manner. And Cooper and I bantered. He was funny. We were funny together — his wisecracks were evenly matched by my comebacks and vice versa — and timed perfectly. They never hurt my feelings like Hubbell's had so many times. Hubbell may not have outright lied to me, but he told me half-truths. A lie by omission is still a lie.

I remembered our first Valentine's Day together when Hubbell devoured me. I teased him, suspecting he broke a lot of hearts in high school. His reply was, "You have no idea, Dakota — it was my heart that was broken." He actually was right — I had no idea about 'Connecticut girl.' They were high school sweethearts, and her family moved to Connecticut after graduation, which separated them — eventually breaking them apart after giving the long-distance relationship a try. I admit I was curious. How did she know Grandma died? Had Dr. and Mrs. Cavanaugh called her since she was a part of their son's life for five years? Was she included in the family's getaways, too?

"What did I ever do to your parents to make them not accept me?" I asked solemnly.

"They like you, Dakota," he stated flatly, not sounding convincing in the least.

"Yeah? But they've never made me feel fully welcome." I wasn't sure if I should even tell Hubbell about his dad's phone call, warning me not to get pregnant. But maybe Hubbell knew already and was even standing in the room when his dad had called me.

"That's your problem if you feel that way, not theirs," he stated coldly.

See? There he goes again, turning it around. I decided to take the high road.

"You're right, Hubbell. I'm the only one in charge of my feelings." I gave a heavy sigh. "I'm happy Laura came back into your life and was there for you at Grandma's funeral. You needed her. Not me."

"You are? You're happy? Not jealous? Not even a little bit?" He sounded so disappointed.

"No. Surprisingly, I'm not jealous." I smiled, feeling confident, knowing my love for Cooper was reciprocated. I just prayed Gloria would fall in love with a super guy at Yale. I didn't think she loved Cooper. At least she had never told me she had fallen in love with him, and she wasn't shy about holding anything back, especially from me. They had been together for about five months. They met at Rhett's bar when she came to visit me over the winter break after Christmas when Hubbell went on vacation to Jamaica with his parents. I was upset and bored, so Luke suggested I throw a party with a few of my friends from school, but most of them were vacationing in Mexico with their folks. But then I thought of Gloria — an old friend from Fort Worth — where I'd lived for sixteen years before moving to Houston shortly after my dad died to live with Luke and Savannah. Gloria wasn't a classmate. She went to a private Jewish day school, but her mom and my mom were friends and crafters — that was how we were thrown together since we were eight years old at their Arts & Crafts night.

The day I called her to see if she wanted to come visit me in Houston wasn't easy. I was nervous — feeling bad that I hadn't returned her last phone call months ago. Of course, it wasn't intentional — I was busy and had a lot on my mind, but as soon as we spoke again, we picked up where we had left off. Gloria didn't plant a guilt trip on me at all. My mom used to tell me that was a sign of a good friendship.

Gloria had gotten a fake ID and was psyched to try it out, so I took her to the only place I knew where they wouldn't question its authenticity. Rhett's was a dump, but it accepted college ID as valid for drinking. A bunch of seniors I knew hung out there on Saturdays, pretending to be juniors at Texas Southern University. A kid named Joey Miller hooked them up — his mom worked in admissions, so he had access to the ID-making machine. Of course, there was a fee. He didn't just do this out of the kindness of his heart. He charged two hundred dollars per ID. He made a killing. Said he was saving up for a Nissan 300 ZX. I felt Cooper eyeing me that initial evening at Rhett's, but somehow Gloria's seduction ignited him into asking her for her phone number. But did he only use Gloria to get to me?

My father had told me during one of his talks, "Love will find you, and when it does, you'll know. You'll feel at peace."

It was true. Since I let "I love you" slip from my mouth, I felt as if a part of me was set free. But now, I was faced with Gloria's feelings. I didn't want anything to come between us. I wanted her friendship ... and I wanted her boyfriend. I tried convincing myself I had been through a lot and deserved to have my cake and eat it, too. But the other part of me was feeling as frustrated as a leashed dog with a squirrel running by.

"I always told you, Dakota, that you were very mature for your age. You're handling this well." Hubbell was making it sound as if this was the end.

"You might have mentioned it once or twice," I said. "But Hubbell," I sighed, "I knew our relationship wouldn't last with you so far away at med school."

"Do you think it would have lasted if I chose a med school in Texas?"

"Maybe. But we'll never know, will we?"

"No. I guess not," he said.

"Did you choose Yale because your dad's an alum, or did you choose it for Laura?"

"I never thought of Laura when I applied. I did it to make my dad proud. She broke up with me just before the start of her sophomore year at Trinity. Never returned to Texas. After her internship her senior year, she was offered a great job upon graduating."

Hubbell paused as if he were waiting for me to say something like, "Wow!" What I really wanted to say was "Whoop-de-doo!" Instead, I just gave an "uh-huh." My initial curiosity about Laura fizzled.

Listening to Hubbell drone on about her made me realize I didn't care what line of work she was in.

"Laura works for Pratt and Whitney. Have you heard of them?"

I felt like pretending I hadn't, but answered truthfully, "Yup. The brains behind the Black Hawk helicopter." I remembered my dad talking about it at supper, and the magazine it was featured in sat in our bathroom for years.

"Very good, Dakota."

He waited as if he wanted me to say thanks. I didn't, of course.

"Laura lives in East Hartford — not New Haven."

"That's not far. Less than an hour," I added.

He sounded impressed. "Didn't know you knew the state so well."

I had looked into Connecticut when I found out Hubbell was accepted at Yale. "I don't think you could do anything to make your dad not proud of you."

"Thanks, Dakota. That's really nice of you to say."

It was nice of me, but it was true. He was their only child, and they worshipped the ground he walked on. Just then, my cell clicked. It was Uncle Travis.

"Hubbell, I have to go. Uncle Travis is on the other end. I haven't talked to him since I left for Rockport."

"Okay. I'll call you later," he said and ended the call.

I don't know why he'd call me later. We were broken up, and there was nothing more to say. Did he still want to be friends? I never understood how people could have a harmonious, platonic relationship with their exes. I think I would feel awkward. But I hoped Gloria was open-minded to it since I wanted both her and Cooper in my life.

Chapter 13

Breakfast For Dinner

"HI, UNCLE TRAVIS!"

"Hi there, Sunshine. It's good to hear your voice. How was your trip?"

I loved how he called me Sunshine. My dad used to call me that, and since his passing, my uncle took over.

"Incredible," I answered truthfully, despite Hubbell and me breaking up.

"Did you walk the Freedom Trail and see Paul Revere's house?"

"There wasn't enough time. But we did go to Faneuil Hall."

"Ah yes, good ol' Quincy Market — great food."

"Yeah, and the street performers were awesome." Part of me wanted to tell my uncle the whole truth.

"I'll be in Houston mid-week for business. I'll take y'all out to dinner — including your Hubbell — okay? Give Savannah a big hug and kiss for me."

"Will do. Can't wait to see you."

"Same here, Sunshine."

"Da...ko...ta!" Savannah was calling from downstairs.

"What? I'm in my room. If you want me, come here!" I hollered back, emulating my mother.

"Will you watch me in the pool?"

"Coming," I hollered back and warned, "Don't go in till I get there!"

Even though I didn't have to remind her, I always did. For the most part, Savannah did as she was told, especially when it came to the pool. I quickly put on my swimsuit and decided to leave my cell phone behind. Whoever phoned would just have to wait. I wanted to play with Savannah without any interruptions. She was a great kid, and pretty soon, I'd be moving into a dorm. Amber Lee encouraged me to live on campus even though the university was only about twenty miles away. She wanted me to get the full college experience. I knew she was right. My guidance counselor at school gave me the same advice. If I didn't like it, I could move back home and commute, but if I didn't try, I'd never know.

It was about three o'clock in the afternoon when Amber Lee joined us out by the pool. She had taken a two-hour nap after lunch. The only complaint she shared concerning being pregnant was feeling more tired than usual. She swore if she didn't nap every day, she felt irritable and acted cranky, which wasn't true, in my opinion. Amber Lee was one of the most bright-eyed and bushy-tailed people I knew, regardless of adequate sleep.

Amber Lee had cut back her hours at work after she made a hefty profit selling her condominium. Luke also told her she didn't have to work if she didn't want to because his pool company was doing incredibly well. He had bought it six years prior, changed its name to Lockwood Pools, and gave Cooper's advertising agency a shot at creating a commercial for it. Because of Cooper's catchy slogan, *"Getting Wet Is Half The Fun!"* business had doubled, so much so that Luke was looking into hiring more employees. Recently, he had even asked me to work for him answering the phones. Naturally, I told him I would. Luke asked very little of me and was always there for me. Doing some office work for him was the least I could do, and besides, I hadn't looked for a job anywhere else.

Savannah was sitting on the pool's second step, playing. In one hand, she held the realistically-sized rubber lobster I had brought her back from Rockport, and in the other, she held Barbie. She was fixated on making Barbie ride the lobster, but the doll kept toppling over. But Savannah didn't give up — she was determined to make it balance. In between her unsuccessful attempts and not showing any signs of frustration, she sweetly asked, "Mommy, what are we having for dinner?"

Immediately Amber Lee and I looked at each other, bug-eyed. We were shocked she had called Amber Lee 'Mommy.' This was her first time, and I wasn't sure if it was intentional or by accident.

Amber Lee decided not to make a big deal over it. She looked at her watch. "It's not even four yet. Are you hungry?"

"I'm so hungry I could eat a horse!" Savannah bellowed. Since I had started reading the Amelia Bedelia book series to her, Savannah's use of idioms had expanded. Because she laughed so hard at the totally naïve, literal-minded, well intentioned but mishap-causing housekeeper, Amelia, I couldn't read them at bedtime — fearful that she'd giggle herself into a second wind.

"Well, I'm eating for two, so I'm always hungry." Amber Lee tapped at her belly and asked, "What do you feel like having, Savannah?"

"I feel like pancakes," Savannah answered. "Boo Berry pancakes." She was still unable to pronounce the letter L.

"That's funny — you don't look like blueberry pancakes!" I playfully interrupted, drawing out the "L."

Luke was planning to ask Savannah's teacher about this once the new school year started. I suggested he look in the yellow pages for a speech pathologist, but he felt it could wait. I think he thought it sounded cute, which it does. But honestly, I have yet to come across anything that Savannah does that isn't both funny and angelic. Most of the time, I just want to gobble her up. My parents used to say this to me when I was a small child, and I vowed I'd never say this to any kid. However, my niece is deliciously cute, and since she came into my life, I now understand the analogy. As her loving aunt, I was worried this speech impediment could be detrimental if it didn't naturally go away. Once her peers catch the way she pronounces certain words, they might tease her. As much as kids were lovable, they could be cruel. Amber Lee and I definitely were concerned and often reminded Luke about it. He promised he'd see to it mid-August.

"I'm not a boo-berry pancake!" Savannah giggled back. "I want to eat 'em."

"Of course you're not a boo-berry pancake," Amber Lee declared, mimicking Savannah. Then, looking in my direction, she playfully added, "Dakota, haven't you been paying attention? We're talking dinner plans!"

"Right. Sorry, Mom!" I teased back.

"She's not your mommy. She's my new mommy." Savannah said with certainty.

"She is?" I asked. I could see the gleam in Amber Lee's eyes. This truly made her happy. But I wanted to know about how this played out with Savannah's actual mom. Obviously, Janet knew Luke had remarried, but I wondered how she felt about their daughter calling the new wife 'Mommy.' When I had met Janet, my first impression of her wasn't positive. For one, she didn't even say, *I'm sorry to hear the passing of your father.* She actually introduced herself as Janet Powers-Trenton with a firm handshake! This was at their house. She didn't come to the funeral. Luke had brought Savannah instead. I was a dinner guest, and their dog jumped up on me, causing me to accidentally toss my glass of grape juice right on Janet! She was furious. And I had to bite my cheek to keep from laughing at her wretched state. But inwardly, I was giddy and thought — serves her right for just handing me this children's beverage without asking me what I'd like to drink. She continued to rant, "I hate your dog!" before she stormed off to change out of her purple-stained linen dress. But I knew there was a lot more she was angry about than this mishap.

I asked, "Savannah, would your mommy in New York be sad if she heard you call Amber Lee 'Mommy'?"

"It was her idea," Savannah answered, as if we should have known this already.

"It was?" Amber Lee asked. "Your mommy wants you to call me 'Mommy' too?" she said, holding her heart, looking as if this notion was so unbelievable.

And truthfully, it was. We were both pleasantly surprised by this. This had to have been the second-nicest thing Janet has ever done for this family. The first, of course, was giving Luke full custody of their daughter. I really thought she'd play Amber Lee up as the evil stepmother and fill Savannah's head with all sorts of nonsense, but it was just the opposite. Not only was Janet willing to share her role, but also her title.

"Are we gonna have breakfast for dinner?" Luke playfully called as he walked from the driveway. "I love that!"

"I didn't even hear your car," Amber Lee said as she tilted her head up.

Luke automatically planted a kiss on her lips, placing his hand on her belly for a rub and asking, "How's the little guy doing today."

They didn't know the sex of the baby, but Luke was certain it was going to be a boy.

Amber Lee teased, "She had the hiccups and woke me from my nap."

"Shame on him," he teased back.

I smiled at their whimsy. Luke and Amber Lee were adorable — totally the opposite of how Luke and Janet were. Janet was so standoffish towards Luke and short-tempered — never easing up or pretending to be appreciative, even for Savannah's sake. Luke's love was sincere and romantic. He was a genuine sweetheart, just like my dad was. Amber Lee saw a good thing and scooped him up. I couldn't imagine Luke being single for long.

I was grateful Janet made this transition for her daughter so easy. Most everyone knows divorce sucks! And usually, there's no *one* real winner. Primarily this parting harms the children, if there are any. And in this case, there was one. Savannah. Savannah seemed okay even though there were a lot of changes for her. First, me — Auntie Dakota — whom none of them knew existed before my dad and Luke's mom died. Then after her parents' quick divorce, she moved to another house with her dad while her mom's new place was an apartment in New York. Then shortly after that, her dad remarried, and a baby sibling was on the way! Besides her mom moving a three-hour plane ride away, these changes were positive. Savannah was the perfect example of the adage that children are resilient.

Chapter 14

Gloria Phones

WHEN I RETURNED to my room after Savannah had fallen asleep, my phone was ringing. I saw that it was Gloria. As soon as I said hello, she blurted out with excitement in her voice.

"Oh my God. You're not going to believe this. Guess who's coming to stay with us for the summer?" She didn't let me guess. "A gorgeous, sexy, French guy from France!"

"You sure this French guy is from France?" I asked sarcastically. "And how do you know he's gorgeous and sexy?"

"I saw his Facebook profile."

She answered in a way that I could tell she was smiling — ecstatic, like when Cooper first phoned her. Wait a minute. "What about Cooper?" I asked, also smiling, feeling relieved. Could this be it? Would Gloria be the one to break up with Cooper? Would he pretend to be crushed and agree it was for the best?

"Wait. I didn't tell you the best part," she continued, ignoring my 'what-about-Cooper' question. "He's Jewish!"

"Your parents must be thrilled! When's the wedding?"

"When I finish at Yale!" she joked back.

"What about Cooper?"

"It seems since our weekend away in Rockport, he's grown distant."

I was speechless but murmured, "Hmm," allowing her to continue.

"I knew it wasn't going to last long, with me heading to Yale in a few months. But I thought our breakup wouldn't be until right before my Yale departure, like maybe the night before my flight."

She sounded pretentious over her acceptance to the Ivy League school, and I wanted to wring her neck for it.

"But now that Frenchie's coming, I don't really care."

"First of all, do not call him Frenchie. I can only picture the ditz from the movie, *Grease*, who dyed her hair pink. And second, when are you going to break this news to Cooper — telling him how you feel?"

"All right, I'll just call him by his first name, which is sexy in itself." In a sultry French accent, she said, "Pierre."

I couldn't help but laugh until she annoyingly added, "That's Peter in French."

Oh my God, did she just say that? Do I have to remind her I'm in AP French? Besides, most everyone knows Pierre is French for Peter, regardless.

"Dakota, why do you care when I break the news to Cooper unless you want him to cry on your shoulder? Although I don't think he will. Cry that is."

"What? Why do you say that?" I asked, trying to sound composed.

"I'd be lying, Dakota, if I pretended otherwise."

"I'm confused."

An awkward silence grew between us for a few seconds, but it felt like forever.

"Dakota, I see the way Cooper looks at you."

"We share pretty heavy commonalities," I reminded. "We both lost our parents, and now his grandfather is slowly dying from cancer like my mom did."

"Would you be upset if Hubbell and I dated? We have a few things in common, too."

"Besides Yale, what else do you have in common with Hubbell?"

"Our exes have fallen for one another."

Shit! She deserved the truth. I didn't deny it. "How long have you known?"

"Since I borrowed someone's binoculars on the beach and saw you two lying close to one another on the raft, acting like a couple in love."

I knew Gloria would hunt down someone with binoculars. I was a little relieved she didn't see the moment when we kissed. I only thought of asking a stupid question, "Why'd you borrow binoculars? Did you want to see if we made it there safely?" Like I cared at this point.

"I saw a yacht and wanted to check it out. You know, see if there were any cute guys aboard," she said lightheartedly. Regardless of being in a relationship, Gloria remained an insatiable flirt and was always looking and admiring. "Then the raft came into view," she said solemnly, "and I saw you two kiss."

So she did see. How could she remain so blasé when we returned to shore?

"Gloria, I'm so sorry. I didn't mean for any of this to happen."

"I know that. It just did, right?" Gloria sounded surprisingly composed. But then she asked with more acid in her voice, "How long have you two been going at it?"

"What?"

"You can tell me. I won't be mad."

How could she not be mad? I answered truthfully, "Gloria, I would never do that."

"When, then? When did you fall for one another?" she asked. I assumed she meant when was our first physical contact.

"At my old home in Fort Worth," I answered.

"I believe you," she said with a deep sigh. "Since then, Cooper hasn't been the same. When he began telling me the story of how he helped you, he sounded as if he was already guilty. He explained how it was in his nature to stop and assist. It's true. I remember we were almost late for the movies because he stopped and offered to help a lady with a flat tire, but then thank God her brother showed up in the nick of time, so we didn't miss the trailers. Anyway, Cooper nearly blew a gasket seeing that it was your car on the interstate with 'smoke billowing' from your hood. 'It was Dakota,' he had said, sounding ecstatic. I was thrilled, too, when he told me. Not thrilled that your car broke down — I was relieved that he was there — at the right time and place. It must have been scary for you. I wouldn't want to be in the breakdown lane on the interstate. Who knows what mutants would stop? Anyway, what a small world."

"Yeah. I was surprised, too," I agreed.

"Unless, of course, he was following you, making sure you made it to Fort Worth safely. God knows your brother was worried like a father, and seeing how Cooper was worked up about you biking by yourself in Rockport, I wondered."

"What? Cooper wasn't following me to Fort Worth. He was headed to Dallas to visit his grandparents. His grandfather was sick. It was purely a coincidence," I said convincingly, and I really hoped it was a fluke because I did not want a relationship where the male was possessive. Then I reminded her, "His grandfather's dying, you know — of cancer," hoping to change the subject.

"I know. It's terrible." And she started to cry.

So much for trying to head our conversation in another direction. I swiftly assured her, "I wasn't lying to you that morning you left my house after my uncle was out of the ICU. I really do consider you like a sister, Gloria. You have become a part of my new family, and I don't want to lose another family member. Gloria, please say it's all right and that you're alright with Cooper and me." I prayed she wouldn't ask if there was an ultimatum. I hated what if's …

There was a brief silence, but I knew she hadn't hung up — I could hear faint music playing in the background. Ironically it was Carly Simon's, *Anticipation*. Meekly I called, "Gloria?"

"I've gotta go," she said, ending the call.

* * *

Let's just say my sleep that night was restless, and then when I did finally fall into a deep sleep, I was awakened by my cell phone at 7 AM. It was Gloria. She started in again without even a simple hello or 'good morning.'

"Dakota, you've been through a lot. If this is what you want ... my Cooper... he's all yours." I could tell she was smiling. "He already lives four hours away from me, and it's a struggle getting together — can you imagine what it'd be like with me in Connecticut? At least you two live in Houston. You deserve one another. I mean that sincerely."

"Really?" I asked with exuberance. This was the answer I had been waiting for.

"Besides, no boy could ever break me away from my one and only sista!" She spoke with conviction.

I laughed. Gloria was and always will be my old friend from Fort Worth, and since moving from there, it felt like the distance made us closer, like long-lost sisters reunited.

"Go on Facebook and check out Pierre Estienne!" she said, her typical bubbly self. "I've gotta run and kick some ass!"

"What?"

"Kickboxing class at the JCC. Bye!"

And click, Gloria was gone before she heard me say, "Have fun!"

I felt a thousand pounds lighter, and instead of falling back to sleep, I decided to get out of bed and go see what Savannah was up to.

Chapter 15

Cooper Phones

"COME OVER," Cooper said without even a hello. He sounded in control, not desperate. "I need you. Come over," he repeated.

"Okay," was all I said. I needed him, too. I assumed Gloria had broken up with him.

I quietly walked into the family room where Luke, Amber Lee, and Savannah were nestled on the large sectional sofa, finishing up the movie, *Despicable Me,* even though Savannah had already fallen asleep. Between them was Paddington Bear — its head was resting on Amber Lee's growing belly as if it were listening to the baby's heartbeat. They looked like the perfect family.

"I'm heading out for a bit," I said lightly.

Luke looked at his watch. "But it's almost ten," he said sensibly.

"That's early, Grandpa," joked Amber Lee. "Don't forget, she's a young'un. Ten's early. I remember when my college roommate and I would nap so we would be ready to par...tay!"

"Don't give her any ideas."

Amber Lee smiled, and with total approval, said, "Have fun!"

Then my brother had to ruin it and ask, "Where are you and Hubbell headed?"

They still did not know about my breakup with Hubbell. I hadn't lied about anything to my brother, and suddenly I came face-to-face with a dilemma. I felt a gnawing sensation — a feeling of guilt — and I wanted to answer, "To Cooper's," but felt funny. Then again, I wanted them to know Cooper and I were an item now. I thought now was the perfect time to just come right out with it.

"I'm headed to Cooper's," I said hurriedly.

"Oh. I didn't know Gloria was in town," Amber Lee said, sounding disappointed that Gloria hadn't paid a visit.

"She's not," I answered.

"Oh," Amber Lee said and then looked immediately at Luke, giving the proverbial deer-caught-in-headlights-look. She nudged him to enquire.

Luke carefully and slowly reached for the TV's remote control so as not to wake Savannah, whose head was resting on his lap. He turned down the volume and asked with concern in his voice, "Is Hubbell there?"

"No."

"What then? Cooper's having a party?" Luke questioned, giving a 'this-is-getting-weirder' look matching the one Amber Lee still had plastered on her clean, makeup-free face.

"No. Just me," I answered, looking down at my shoes.

"Do you think that's a good idea? You going over to Cooper's... alone?" he asked calmly.

"Hubbell and I broke up in Boston. He's back with his old girlfriend. She showed up at his grandma's funeral," I blurted out nervously. Then stupidly added as if it made a difference, "She's from Connecticut."

"I'm sorry," Amber Lee consoled, shaking her head in disbelief. She seemed slightly offended that I hadn't confided in her earlier. "Is that why he chose Connecticut for med school?" She had to ask.

"Who knows?" I shrugged. Then I anxiously stammered, "And Gloria and Cooper broke up!" I waited for them to take that bit of news in, too, before I added somewhat meekly, "Cooper and I love each other."

They looked completely shocked and puzzled as if they had just received bad news but then were told not to worry. At that moment, I wanted to reconfirm that, but I hated those two words. Practically everyone told me that when my mom was first diagnosed with cancer. Don't worry, they said. She's a survivor. She'll pull through. What did they know? They were wrong. And ever since then, I've hated the "Don't worry" cliché.

Amber Lee began petting Paddington as if it was a live animal, and Luke was smoothing down Savannah's hair. They both seemed nervous and remained staring at me, somewhat bug-eyed. I pictured imaginary clouds over their heads with *Please Explain* written on them.

"What do you mean?" Amber Lee asked, sounding a little bit like she was going to cry. She didn't like controversy, friction, or making waves, and this was starting to sound like a storm a' brewing.

"Gloria suspected it. She told me she's all right with it," I explained. "The Golds are hosting a French student — supposedly a hottie, according to Gloria. She was already planning on breaking up with Cooper to be free, so she can have fun with Pierre!" I finished, sounding all cheery to break the solemnness.

"So y'all are just going to continue on 'double dating' but with new partners?" Amber Lee asked with furrowed brows.

"Yeah. I guess so," I answered. Although how she put it made it sound so weird — almost cult-like, as if Gloria and I were hippies, open to sharing partners or worse — that 'friends with benefits' fad.

"What do you mean 'Gloria suspected it'? How long has this been going on between you and Cooper?" Luke asked

"Since he drove me to Fort Worth," I answered and then asked irritably, "Can I go now, or is there more to this inquisition?"

"Dakota, we don't mean to pry. We just love you so much. We don't want to see you get hurt or people you love get hurt," Amber Lee explained, sounding very sincere. "We want you to be happy."

"I *am* happy," I gently reminded her. "Gloria's good. She gave me her blessing. She wants me to be happy. Cooper makes me happy."

They said nothing but gave a closed-mouth smile in unison.

"Okay? I'm gonna go now."

"Okay," Luke said.

"Say hello from us," Amber Lee called.

As I was getting into my car, Luke appeared. "What now?" I asked, feeling he may have changed his mind and that his initial okay wasn't okay anymore.

"Just wanted to let you know, Dakota, you have a hall pass — there's no curfew tonight."

I think my jaw dropped.

He explained why. "I know where you'll be. You'll be safe — at Cooper's — with Cooper. He's a good guy, Dakota...but just take it slow."

"Okay," was all I said, but then he added as he always did in situations like this, "I trust you, Dakota, to make the right decisions."

As I drove away, I felt emotionally relieved but also drained, and I just wanted to melt in Cooper's arms and fall asleep. I was surprised but also grateful Luke said I could spend the night at Cooper's. I was looking forward to it.

Chapter 16

Winter Morning

IMMEDIATELY COOPER swallowed me up. My face was in his chest, and already I felt better. His scent was my aromatherapy.

He breathed in my loose hair, his hands roaming my backside as he whispered in my ear, "God, you feel so good."

He led me in, holding my hand. Brought me to the sofa and told me to sit.

"What am I, a dog?" I joked

"Only the most adorable," he answered as he went into the kitchen, which was visible from the living room. A three-foot wall with a granite countertop separated the two rooms and acted as a bar. *Architectural Digest, Time, Smithsonian, Newsweek,* and finally — there it was, *Sports Illustrated* — were spread out in a fan-like pattern on his oversized glass coffee table.

He returned, carefully carrying two mugs.

"Yum. Hot chocolate." Before I took a sip, "With mini marshmallows, too? You rock!"

He smiled and told me how adorable I was. I was only three sips in when he stood and said, "Follow me."

"Are you sure you don't mean, 'Come here, girl'?"

"Come here, girl," he teased as he walked to the back, which I remembered was where his bedroom was. He had made the other bedroom on the opposite side into an office.

I followed him, feeling somewhat uncertain, remembering Luke's advice to take it slow. On the drive over, I contemplated my brother's words of wisdom and had decided I didn't want to go to bed with Cooper just yet. I'd craved him for months, and now was my chance to devour him, but my conscience was telling me otherwise.

Then I saw it. I saw why he wanted me in his bedroom. It was staring right at me before I even entered. The painting I had admired back in Rockport hung opposite his bed. Cooper had noticed the effect *Winter Morning* had on me and bought it!

"Oh my God," I softly uttered. A dreamy thought glazed over my conscience: I could wake up to this — him and *Winter Morning* — every morning. He'd keep me warm, safe from the beckoning waves that came alive. I pictured us walking hand and hand, skirting the cold water during the off-season months — Cooper's favorite time to go and walk the beach.

Cooper surprised me, quoting Ralph Waldo Emerson: "'The landscape belongs to the person who looks at it'…I'm sure seascapes apply."

I turned my attention to him. "It's beautiful," I said, looking into his eyes.

"It's for you." He looked into my eyes, into the inside of me.

I could feel tears welling up. My mother often said how the most beautiful things in life are unexpected. I managed to utter, "What?"

Cooper stepped closer to me. He took my mug from my hands and placed it on the tall dresser behind me.

I remembered the price — three thousand dollars. "Cooper…it's too much. I can't accept it," I said, shaking my head slowly — taking it all in — overwhelmed by the feeling that this was the most romantic thing in the world. Buying art to express one's love.

"Then don't. You'll just have to come into my bedroom every time you want to admire it," he said with a mischievous grin.

I melted. I kissed him with all the passion I had building up in my five-foot-six body. We moved together, stepping closer to his bed. As soon as my heels touched the bed's edge, he leaned me back onto it. Our heated bodies shimmied up until our heads were buried in the pillows. His body pressed against mine, making me feel incredibly excited, as if I was on fire. I just wanted him to free me of my clothes, and I wanted to rip his off! The plush comforter was blanketing us as we were entwined in each other's arms. But then he stopped. His breathing was heavy, as if he had just run a marathon. He moved slightly off me. I moved, too. We were on our sides facing each other.

"What? What's wrong?" I asked, also sounding short-winded.

His deep brown eyes looked into mine. "I want to take it slow," he said softly.

What? Did Luke call you? I wanted to joke but knew Cooper was serious.

"I love you, Dakota, and, believe me, I desperately want to show you just how much, but tonight's not the night. Gloria just broke up with me, and I don't want to be making love to her best friend on the rebound."

I was hesitant to tell him I already knew and that she had called me, but my conscience told me I should.

"Cooper, Gloria phoned me first. She told me she felt you were acting distant. She knew it wasn't going to last between you two once she went off to college — like you thought, too." I didn't dare tell him about Pierre. "And she saw us kissing on the raft. She knows about us."

"What?" He sounded in complete shock.

"She didn't tell you?"

"No!"

"Why are you upset? This is what we wanted."

"We didn't do anything really but kiss, Dakota," he said, slightly agitated. Then he gave a heavy sigh. "Did you tell her that I told you I loved you?" He repositioned himself, letting go of my hand, and moved slightly away from me, looking up at the ceiling, waiting for my response. It was like he was silently praying I had kept my mouth shut about that.

"No," was all I said, but inwardly I was crying, *but you do…you do love me, don't you?*

I suddenly felt vulnerable lying on Cooper's bed. Thank God we weren't nude; that would've made it more awkward.

"Good," he said. "She doesn't need to know how I feel about you…that'd only hurt her more."

More? Honestly, I don't think Gloria is feeling too hurt. She's already excited about Pierre's visit. I inwardly cringed. "Okay," I replied slowly. But Cooper was right — Gloria didn't need to know he whispered those magical three words to me when they were still an item.

"What time do you need to be home?" he asked.

"One o'clock," I lied.

He looked at his watch. "We could watch a movie," he said.

"Would you be upset if I went home?" I wanted this night to end. Starting off a relationship like this couldn't be good. Perhaps our five-year age gap did make a difference. Cooper was the experienced one. I lost my virginity to Hubbell six months ago and am painstakingly learning the ups and downs of romance.

Chapter 17

Uncle Travis Visits

WHEN LUKE and I pulled in, finally home from a very long but busy eight-hour shift at Lockwood Pools, we were pleasantly surprised to see Uncle Travis' pristine Jag in our driveway.

"Holy cow! Uncle Travis is here — I completely forgot!" I cried.

"What do you mean?" Luke asked.

"We talked last week, and he had mentioned he had business in Houston and would stop by — take us out to dinner. Maybe even Ronda's Rodeo Road House."

"Remember the last time we ate there with him? I thought he was going to leave with the waitress," he laughed.

"Yeah, I remember. I remember how blatant she was, bending over him," I answered, returning the chuckle.

"Oh yeah," Luke said, smirking as if he were visualizing the waitress's bosom.

Amber Lee and Uncle Travis were lying on lounge chairs by the pool as Savannah did the dog paddle from one side of the shallow end to the other. Uncle Travis looked relaxed, drinking a cold beer, and Amber Lee was enjoying one of her homemade, organic fruit smoothies.

"Daddy! Aunt Dakota!" Savannah bellowed as she toddled up the stairs.

I held a towel open for her, wrapped her in it, and swooped her up. "I am so proud of my little mermaid!"

Savannah giggled her infectious giggle.

"Pass the cannoli!" Luke called.

I gingerly carried her over to Luke's awaiting arms then turned my attention toward my uncle, who was now standing up and waiting. With affection, he cooed, "My sweet, sweet Dakota. Oh, how I missed you."

We hugged.

He looked me up and down, grinning. "I swear, child, every time I see you, you're more and more beautiful. You look just like your mother; God rest her soul."

"And I do declare, you look as handsome as I last remember — minus a few pounds!" I returned earnestly.

"Seven pounds," he answered proudly and then tugged at his belt. "A notch smaller!"

"That's fantastic." I smiled.

"What are we doing for dinner? I'm starvin'," Amber Lee interrupted, rubbing her belly, which was accentuated even more in her emerald green swimsuit. "I could go for a slab of baby back ribs, fried chicken, sweet potato, and a side of coleslaw."

"That's all?" Luke teased

"Sounds good to me. Let's head over to Rhonda's — my treat," Uncle Travis said.

"Yum." Amber Lee said as she held out her hand. "Let's go get changed, Savannah." As soon as Luke unwrapped Savannah, the two of them tootled away adorably, holding hands.

Luke and I stayed behind with Travis.

Luke asked as he headed towards the outdoor fridge, "Want another Bud Light, Travis?

"No, thanks."

Luke handed me a cold Pepsi. He opened his can of beer and declared, "This is a nice surprise."

"It's great to see everyone," Uncle Travis said, smiling from ear to ear.

"Are we going to meet Pamela and Alexis at Rhonda's?" Luke asked, sliding onto one of the lounge chairs.

"No," Uncle Travis answered without offering further explanation.

Luke and I looked at each other, a bit surprised, as if we had said something wrong. Uncle Travis saw our look of worry and immediately clarified but gave a heavy sigh as if he needed a whole new breath. "Pamela is a beautiful, spectacular woman, and *young*." He emphasized 'young.' "She wants another kid, which is understandable, but not up my alley."

"Her biological clock is ticking?" I assumed.

"Yes. Time is valuable. That's why I don't feel any animosity towards her breaking up with me. She deserves to have a second child, and it would be great for Alexis, too. I just can't be the guy to father it — I'm past my prime. It wouldn't be fair to the child to have a dad people would mistake for a grandpa," he finished.

Luke looked solemn, the same way he did when I tried explaining how Cooper was transitioning from Gloria over to me. Thank goodness Amber Lee wasn't here, or else she might cry.

Travis continued, "I know in the past when I've come to town, I have stayed at the Saint Regis Hotel, and then at Pamela's when we were all hot and heavy, but if you don't object." He looked at Luke and me with doleful eyes, "I'd like to stay here — be with family."

I was just taken aback that he actually used the terminology 'hot and heavy.'

Luke answered, coming out of his brief dismay, "Of course. Of course, you can always stay here. You never need an invite." Then he added in Spanish, "Mi casa es su casa."

"Thanks, Luke. I surely do appreciate that."

But I wasn't completely buying his all-of-a-sudden-wanting-to-stay-with-family attitude. I stood up from my chair, walked right over to my uncle, bent down so our faces were level, and placed my hands on his chair's armrests. Penning him in, I looked into his sad eyes and asked boldly, "Is something wrong? You're not sick or anything? You'd tell me, right?" I remembered how my parents hid my mom's cancer from me until it became noticeable that something was amiss.

* * *

I was nine. My mom and I were in the bathroom together, sharing the mirror. I was trying on headbands and asking her opinion: the black one with white polka dots or the glittery one with the rhinestone bow. She smiled and told me that both looked good on me, then asked what shoes I was going to wear because that would make a difference. Then she smiled and said whichever one I wasn't going to wear, she would, and we'd be headband twins! As she called us the 'headband twins,' a large chunk of her hair came out onto the brush we also shared. I freaked. Staring at her new bald spot, I screamed as if she were being murdered.

My dad had run in, yelling, "What's happening?" but when he saw my mother's eyes well up as she held the brush with a clump of her hair dangling from it, all he could say was, "Oh," sounding as if he knew this day would come.

My mother sat on the closed toilet seat and motioned me to sit on her lap. I did. My dad knelt next to us, and the two of them explained as if they were telling a story and each played a character, like Frog and Toad, but in this case, their story had a fatal ending. Mom told me her chemotherapy treatments were making her hair fall out, and it would only be a matter of weeks before she would be bald. She pooh-poohed my sad face, tenderly holding it with both her hands and telling me she desperately needed my opinion, and asked if it would be okay with me if I skipped school that day so the three of us could shop for a wig.

We shuffled into the car and drove to Wigs by Gladys, where the proprietor was known to actually name his wigs after famous persons whose hair was similar — but in his generation. That day I was briefed on who Cher and Dorothy Hamel were. Mom decided to make the best of her situation and lightened the mood by forcing my dad and me to try on wigs

— until the three of us were keeled over in hysterics. Dad looked absolutely ridiculous as Cher, and I thought the Dorothy Hamel wig looked like a bowl cut.

Our laughter was the perfect medicine for my mom that day. Adorably she asked us, in a British accent, no less, "So what should it be, my giggle pusses — the Lady Di?" as she pushed her hair up inside the wig. We (including the shopkeeper) all agreed my mother looked best in the Princess Diana wig.

Afterward, we went out to lunch and carried on our silliness by speaking in British accents. We were so convincing that we even fooled the waitress.

"What part of England are y'all from?" the waitress asked.

Mom and I blushed as Dad confidently answered, "Nottinghamshire."

We had just watched Robin Hood the night before.

We laughed some more, and my dad ordered two glasses of champagne and a Shirley Temple. It was one of the fun times I shared with my parents, despite the circumstances.

* * *

"Dakota, I'm just fine. Do I need to be sick to want to stay with you?" Uncle Travis asked, shaking his head. Then he looked down at my hands, which were still steady on the chair's armrests, and asked, "Can I get up? Please?"

I didn't relent. "Tell me the truth."

"For goodness' sake, Dakota, I am not dying!"

"You promise?"

"As much as I'd like to believe I'm invincible, eventually I'm going to die, Dakota."

"Don't be a wise-ass. You know perfectly well what I mean."

"Yes, I know what you mean. And no, I am not dying — at least not that I know of. Now, let me up!"

As I let go of his chair, Savannah and Amber Lee came out, wearing matching outfits — navy blue dresses with white, sailor-type collars tied with a red bow.

"Oh my God. Is there a cruise y'all are going on we don't know about?" I said.

"You two look so adorable. I am the luckiest man," Luke declared

"You mean *we* are the luckiest men," Uncle Travis corrected as he stood up from his chair and angled his arm for Amber Lee to take hold. "to be escorting these fine ladies to dinner."

Amber Lee took his arm with a big smile and rested her head on it as they promenaded to the car. "Oh, how I missed you, Travis," she said in her sweet Southern drawl. She was so easily charmed by gentlemen. She would have relished living in the Jane Austen era.

"Where in the world did you find a maternity shop that also sells kid's clothes to match?" I asked, trailing behind them.

"I didn't. My mom did. They came today by UPS," she answered. Then asked, "Doesn't Savannah look like Shirley Temple?"

"On the good ship, Lollipop!" Luke sang cheerily.

We all burst into laughter. I hadn't expected this of Luke and was impressed. I wondered if he had watched this old-time classic, Bright Eyes, with his mom, as I had with mine.

I volunteered to sit in the back, facing out of the rear window of the new car Luke had traded Amber Lee's BMW convertible for. "Convertibles are not safe for transportin' babies," Amber Lee declared at breakfast one morning — another piece of info she had learned from some parenting magazine. Supposedly the Volvo was rated 'safest family vehicle.'

Just as we were seated at the roadhouse, that same vivacious young beauty queen cheerleader of a waitress my uncle had been smitten with months prior (but had forgotten her name) pleasantly captured us.

"Well, I'll be! If it isn't Mr. Travis Bernard Kenwood," the waitress announced with a grin as big as the breasts straining the buttons on her shirt.

I saw my uncle take a quick glance at the nametag all the wait staff had to wear. Hers read, *Betsy*, in cursive writing.

"Betsy. My darling. How've you been, dear?"

"I'm just fine right now, at this very moment staring into your daring eyes," she answered as he blushed and, surprisingly, had no rebuttal. She continued with her brazen flirting. "I've missed you. Where've you been?"

Before this goes any further, let me explain. My uncle has made headlines due to all the cases he has won — defending well-to-do people in the public eye. And he was one of the fifteen most eligible bachelors in some Texas magazine a decade ago — probably the time this waitress hit puberty, so she wouldn't have known that tidbit about him.

I remember when my mom had cut the article out and posted it on our fridge, where it stayed for years. It was an incredible photograph of my uncle — professional-looking but not too touched-up. His chin scar from an accident still showed, which Mom thought gave him that sexy, rugged look. And every time he stopped over for a cold beer after work and ended up staying for dinner, he'd tease how we should splurge on a frame so it wouldn't get marred.

My mother equally matched his humor. "We're waitin' on the poster size — to hang above the mantel."

Then my dad would holler back, "Be careful what you wish for, Loretta! Travis might just bring one."

And my uncle would grin, holding his beer in the chilled mug my mom always had on reserve for him, and declare, "Jethro, you are one lucky man, I tell ya!" And then he'd turn to my mom and coo, "Loretta, you just say the word, and I'll whisk you away to some exotic place."

I swear the scene was like a sitcom. Dad knew my mom's and Travis's flirting was all just a playful act — purely innocent and harmless.

I wondered if Betsy was looking at my uncle as her next Sugar Daddy. She came across as that kind. But my uncle was too astute — no one, not even a gorgeous female, could take advantage of him.

Chapter 18

Banana Pancakes

UNCLE TRAVIS moseyed in through the back door into the kitchen, dressed in his suit from yesterday. He held the jacket over his shoulder with two fingers; his wrinkled white shirt was half tucked in, with the rest of it hanging over his rumpled-looking slacks.

"Good morning!" he declared.

"Good morning," I returned and playfully added in a British accent, "You naughty little boy, you."

"Where is everyone? " he asked, slightly blushing.

"Sleeping." I looked at the giant wall clock. "It's only eight o'clock."

"Yeah, so why are you up so early?" he asked as he placed his jacket over the back of a chair and pulled out a stool.

"I know." I chuckled, "this is a rarity. Why didn't you stay with what's-her-name?"

"Her name's Betsy," he corrected, "and she had a 'spinning class' to go to," he said, sounding clueless.

I laughed and explained, "It's an exercise class where you bike ferociously on a stationary bike with blaring music to get you pumped and psyched as if you could win the Tour de France — burning off a million calories!"

He laughed. "That explains it."

I rolled my eyes. "Please don't describe how insatiable Betsy was in bed."

He did anyway.

"She was crazy!" he sighed, "but I managed to..."

I put my hand in the halt position like a school crossing guard. "Stop!"

A look of pure sexual mischief was plastered on his face, and I couldn't help but laugh. "What'd you expect? She's in her early 20s."

"I'm exhausted!" he confessed.

"What'd you expect?" I repeated. "You're in your late 50s," I chided.

He laughed. I laughed, and then Luke sauntered down the kitchen stairway, asking, "What's so funny?"

Sounding proud, Uncle Travis asked, "Luke, when did Dakota become so wise?" He seemed glad I was no longer naïve.

"When she moved in with me, of course," Luke replied.

I smiled. As always, Luke approached me, giving me a good morning kiss on the top of my head before reaching for his coffee mug. Not only was my brother downright lovable, but he reminded me of my father. In so many ways, Luke was a replica of our dad, Jethro.

"So, Travis, how was last night?" Luke asked.

"Oh my God. I can't believe you just asked him that. He obviously just came home — look at how he's dressed. How do you think his night went?" I answered as if I was a dorm mother.

"I know where he spent the night," Luke said. "Just fishing for details," he added with a sly grin.

"And I thought Gloria was bad," I said, rolling my eyes and muttering under my breath, "Boys," as if they were the world's worse.

Uncle Travis got up to pour himself some coffee. As he scooped in a heaping teaspoon of sugar and stirred, he said mischievously, "She gets off work at midnight, so remind me to take a nap."

Luke laughed. "That good, huh?"

Uncle Travis just nodded.

"Oh my God," I said, rolling my eyes once again, but I still volunteered to make breakfast. "How'd you boys like some banana pancakes?"

"Yes, please!" my uncle cried.

"Sounds good. And bacon too, please," Luke requested.

"For you, yes. But none for you," I said, looking at my uncle. "It's bad enough Betsy may give you a heart attack. I don't need to reinforce it with bacon."

He chuckled without any rebuke and then browsed through the paper as I was getting the ingredients out. It was unbelievable that I was at the point in my life where sex was casual in conversations — and with my uncle, no less.

"Can I get the sports section?" Luke asked. The two sat at the island, looking very content, reading the paper and drinking their coffee as I prepared them a hearty breakfast. I felt fortunate. I may have been stricken by the death of my parents, but I was blessed with a doting uncle and brother, who were both contemporary thinkers. They still held onto traditional values, which I admired, and they loved me unconditionally to the moon and back.

As they were devouring their first round of pancakes, my uncle blurted out, with maple syrup dripping from his chin, "So, Dakota, I hear you're seeing Cooper nowadays."

How clever. He waited until I served him his breakfast before he prodded.

"Yes," I answered and then scolded, "Use your napkin for goodness' sake!" sounding like my mother.

He wiped around his mouth before prying, "Why? Why no longer Hubbell?"

"Hubbell's back with his old girlfriend..." And before I could explain further, my uncle interrupted.

"So Cooper was the next best thing?"

"No!" I answered defensively.

He gave me a disapproving look but said nothing. I explained in a softer tone, "Cooper and I fell for each other months ago, but we kept it a secret so we wouldn't hurt Gloria or Hubbell."

"Those are the worst kinds of relationships," he said, shaking his head. "Dakota, it's not good to go after a friend's lover."

Shoot. I didn't expect this. I wanted his approval. I had high regard for my uncle's opinion. What he said was almost sacred to me, even though at times he was a promiscuous son-of-a-bitch. I knew he was smart as a pistol and was a good reader of people. He never seemed all that thrilled about Hubbell, so I thought he'd be okay with our breakup. He seemed to gravitate more towards Cooper. Perhaps because they had the same blood type, and if it weren't for Cooper, my uncle's hospital stay would have been more arduous.

"Uncle Travis, it's not like that," I said, sliding another pancake onto his plate. "Cooper and I have a lot in common."

"Okay. So you both lost your parents — what else?"

"Why are you acting this way? What do *you* know?" I asked, emphasizing the "you" because his intimate relationships never lasted.

"Dakota, I'm older and wiser."

Then I became suspicious, as if he knew something about Cooper that I didn't.

"Are you hiding something about Cooper? Is there some new evidence about the accident you're keeping from me?" I was tapping the spatula against the counter, waiting for his response.

"Quit it with the spatula — it's making my hangover worse."

"I have a right to know."

"No. I just think it's a bad idea."

Just at that moment, he was saved by the bell — figuratively — Southern belle, Amber Lee, who declared as she waddled down, holding her belly with one hand as if the baby depended on it, "What smells so good? That's what got me out of bed!" She was only four and a half months along but acted like she could give birth any day. Luke went over to help her down from the last step and held her. They embraced and kissed as if they hadn't spooned all night. Talk about insatiable…

Then, when she saw me, she was a bit surprised. "Why, even Dakota's up?"

"Yup! Couldn't sleep late," I said, pouring more batter onto the hot griddle.

"Is everything all right?" But before I could answer, she added, "We'll talk later." Maybe she didn't think my uncle would understand my complicated love life. She apparently didn't know he was already privy to it. She then turned her attention to him. "I didn't expect you to be home this early, Travis," she said, all cutesy-like. "That Betsy's darlin'!"

"She is," he said as he got up from his stool, cleared his plate, and offered, "Sit, sweetheart, and enjoy some of Dakota's delicious pancakes."

As she took his seat and thanked him, I plopped a piping hot banana pancake in front of her. "Yum," she declared. "These look like the best pancakes ever!"

I smiled. "Eat up. There's more where they came from," I said, sounding like my mom again.

I eyed my uncle staring at me. Did he see my mother in me, too? He smiled. "Dakota sure does know how to make the best pancakes." Refilling his mug, he added, "And I believe she knows what she's doing. I trust her to make the right decisions," he finished with a wink.

Amber Lee looked a tad confused. "Okay, what'd I miss?"

"I told Travis that Dakota and Hubbell weren't a couple anymore, but she and Cooper are," Luke informed his wife.

"Honey, you shouldn't have. It's Dakota's business, not yours," Amber Lee lightly reprimanded. "She's capable of telling him herself, in her own time."

"It's okay," I said, coming to Luke's rescue when I saw his sorrowful look, even though his new bride was one hundred percent correct. "I was planning on telling Uncle Travis. It just happened to be sooner rather than later, thanks to my bro. But no worries — it's all good."

Just then, the phone rang.

When I picked up the phone to answer it, Savannah already had. I heard her sweet, tiny voice.

"Uh-huh. He's with me right now." Then she giggled, "Paddington sleeps with me every night, silly!"

"Mine, too!" Cooper spoke.

I smiled even though I knew it wasn't true, unless he had his childhood teddy bear tucked in a drawer or hidden in his walk-in closet.

"I would love to read the story of Paddington Bear to you."

"We're done with that story. Aunt Dakota's reading A...Amei-a Be... Di-a now," Savannah said, trying hard to pronounce the title correctly.

"I love that crazy maid. Can I come over today and read it with you?" Cooper spoke with pure enthusiasm, and I couldn't help but think someday he would make the perfect dad.

"I have to check first...hold on!"

She didn't wait for Cooper to answer as I heard a thud — her receiver hitting the wooden floor.

"Savannah? Savannah!" Cooper called.

I decided to let him know I had picked up.

"Hey, Cooper."

"Hey, doll face. I miss you."

"So you're making dates with my niece?" I teased.

"You, too, of course — she needs a chaperone."

"Okay. And I'll be sure to wear my furry sweater. I've got competition."

"You heard that?"

"Maybe," I drew out the word. "I couldn't disrupt the merriment."

"Are you jealous?"

"A little…but more disappointed you didn't introduce us."

"I would've, but you jumped my bones before I had a chance."

"You didn't seem to mind," I teased. Within a minute, our flirting came to a halt when Savannah came running down the stairs, calling my name, "Dakota!"

"Hold on, Cooper. What's up, cutie patootie?" But when Savannah smelled the pancakes, she completely forgot to tell me about Cooper being on the phone and bellowed, "Yummy! Pancakes!"

"Is there something you want to tell me first?" I asked, laughing, holding the receiver out so Cooper could hear. Savannah shook her head, shinning up onto a stool, completely mesmerized by the smell of pancakes.

"No? Are you sure?" I reiterated. I spoke into the phone, chuckling. "She's shaking her head."

"I can't believe it!" Cooper cried playfully.

I teased, "Do you still want to go out with her? She's already forgotten about you."

"Just as long as you never do," he said. "I'd keel over and die."

Then, as if a light bulb went off, Savannah remembered, "Aunt Dakota, Cooper's on the phone. Can he come over?" She spun around on her stool. "He wants to read with us."

Amber Lee laughed, stopped Savannah's stool from spinning, and greeted, "Good morning, cupcake," and fed her a forkful of her pancake.

Luke took over, flipping the next batch since I was on the phone.

"So, can I come over now? I left a text asking you to call me when you got up. I didn't want to disturb your beauty sleep."

"I got up early and came downstairs — left my cell upstairs. Sorry. Sure, come over. We're not doing anything special today." Then I eyed my uncle looking up from his paper, giving me a look that asked, aren't I special? "Oh, but Uncle Travis is in town. He's staying with us."

"He's not staying at Pamela's?" Cooper asked.

"I'll fill you in later," I answered. "See you soon."

"Can't wait," Cooper said before we hung up.

I couldn't wait either. I was so relieved he wasn't still upset.

Chapter 19

Riding

WHEN COOPER arrived, I was cleaning up after breakfast. Whitney Houston's famous song, I Will Always Love You, was faintly audible from the overhead ceiling speakers. Luke programmed his own anthology of love songs for Amber Lee, and this was one of her favorites. They were all out by the pool. Luke had custom fans built into the large veranda, which allowed us to stay outdoors longer during the summer heat.

Stealthily Cooper came in from behind me, clasping my waist as I stood in front of the kitchen sink, washing the stainless-steel bowl. He pressed up against me and nuzzled the back of my neck, moving his lips to my ear and whispered, "I missed you."

I softly moaned, turned off the faucet, and turned to him.

We kissed passionately. In a matter of seconds, though, we were interrupted by Savannah. She ran in wet from the pool, hurried into the laundry room for something — I couldn't see what it was because she sped right back out again. Cooper and I laughed at how adorable she looked.

"When am I going to get you alone again, Dakota?"

You had me alone, Cooper...at your place, but then you wigged out."

"I'm sorry," he said with pleading eyes. "I didn't expect to feel that way."

"Cooper?" I hesitated and then looked directly into his eyes. "Was it more exciting to be with me behind Gloria's back?"

He firmly held both my hands, looked straight into my eyes, and answered, "No. I hated it."

My first thought was how my mom disliked that word. I wished Cooper came up with a different one.

"What's wrong?" he asked.

"Hate's a strong word. You hated being with Gloria?"

"No. I hated..." He corrected, "I disliked having to pretend."

"Pretend what?"

"Dakota, now you're wigging out."

"Pretend to be in love with my friend for sex?" I finished.

"We never confessed we loved each other because we didn't. It was just about sex and having fun," Cooper stated, starting to sound annoyed with me.

"Sorry if I think two people should love each other before doing it, and that it sounds absurd to you."

"It's different for guys," he stated. Then reminded me, "Your friend didn't seem to mind. If you recall, she was just as brazen as I was the night we met."

I could hear my mom reminding me not to judge, "Everyone's made from a different mold, and you either accept someone for who they are or look past it." It's safe to say my friend Gloria is a nympho and doesn't hide it. She's also blatantly honest and says what's on her mind, and I need to respect her for that. As for boys, my father warned me the male species is only after one thing! He never actually came clean with what that one thing was, but it was safe to assume he meant sex. Dad was just too embarrassed to explain it.

"You're right. I'm sorry, Cooper."

Cooper took the bowl I'd been drying for the past three or so minutes from my hands and teasingly warned, "You may put a hole in it." He placed it on the adjacent counter, along with the dish towel. Stepping closer to me, he leaned in for a kiss. I reciprocated and apologized again. He did, too.

"Let's go riding," I suggested. "You can ride Luke's horse. He's been so busy with work he hasn't been able to exercise Saint Patty, and Amber Lee can't, so I'm sure they'll appreciate it."

"All right, but only if I get to take you out to dinner tonight," he propositioned.

"Uncle Travis is here for the weekend, so we're staying in for a home-cooked meal — you're welcome to join us if you want," I offered. "Then afterward, he's headed to Betsy's."

"Who's Betsy? And what happened to Pamela?"

"Pamela wants a baby. My uncle doesn't. And Betsy's a young waitress at Rhonda's who practically threw herself at him last night."

"How convenient for your uncle," he stated, and then asked the inevitable, "What does he think of us?"

"He thinks I should never go for my friend's leftovers," I answered truthfully.

Cooper looked offended.

"But I told him he wasn't one to give relationship advice. Besides, Amber Lee thinks you're top shelf, and I value her opinion," I shared, smiling, and hoped hearing this would ease his worry.

"She's a smart woman," he stated. Then with a questioning smile, he asked, "Do you even know what top shelf is?"

I laughed, "Yes! My mom used it all the time, referring to my dad as 'the best'!"

He laughed. "Sounds like your parents respected and loved one another incredibly."

"Very much."

"Mine did, too. That's really special, you know? We're truly blessed with that memory."

Chapter 20

Pool Plunge

COOPER AND I were in luck. As we were coming in from riding, Luke and Savannah were heading out. He said he was taking her to Alexis' house for a play date, then running a few errands, and that Amber Lee and Travis were napping.

After having ridden for a little more than an hour, my body was drenched in sweat. It felt so good to sit in the shade of the pool patio and take off my cowboy boots and socks. Cooper followed suit. When I got up to grab us a cold drink from the fridge, Cooper quickly scooped me up and impulsively jumped into the deep end of the pool!

As we came to the surface, we kissed and kissed. We grew tired from treading water, so we swam to the ladder, where I sat on the middle rung. He held onto the handrails, holding me captive. We looked into each other's eyes. His were the color of dark chocolate. He was so seductive − not saying anything took my breath away. I found myself unbuttoning his shirt, peeling it off, throwing it onto the patio while not taking my eyes off him. He smiled at my sudden aggressiveness. My hands returned to his chiseled body. I clawed at his muscular chest and moved down, unbuckling his belt, unzipping him, pushing down his jeans, and used my feet to finish the task − bringing them to the surface with my toes. Then threw them, too, onto the patio.

He laughed. "Very clever, Dakota. Now it's your turn." He told me to lift my arms as he peeled off my T-shirt. He was tempted to unclasp my bra but said with an adorable pout, "Can't. Not here." He continued down my waist and undid my jeans. I helped, shimmying out of them as he pulled them off. My undies came with, but he pulled those up, returning that look of disappointment as he repeated, "Can't. Not here." He was so damn respectful and responsible. Our pile of clothes mounted as we passionately kissed some more. But then slowly, Cooper pushed himself away, telling me in between heavy breaths, "I'm going to burst if you don't stop, Dakota."

I smiled. "Good. My plan is working."

"Come over tonight when your uncle leaves for his new girl's."

"You mean sneak out?"

"No. Tell your brother — just not your uncle."

"Does Travis intimidate you?"

"A little." His answer surprised me, but I was glad he was honest. My uncle had a tendency to browbeat, but I thought Cooper was strong enough to take it. "Let's swim," he finished as he started away from me, probably to ease his erection.

About twenty minutes went by before we climbed out of the pool and walked over to our clothes pile by the ladder and worked together, wringing out our jeans and shirts before I threw them in the machine for a quick wash. He sat with a towel around his waist at the kitchen island, reading the paper.

"I'll be right back. Give me five minutes, and then I'll make us some lunch, okay?" I said.

"Sounds good," he replied without his eyes leaving the page. My uncle was the same way this morning, engrossed in some article.

I headed up, taking the stairs two at a time.

When I bounced back down, dressed in shorts and a tank top, Cooper immediately asked, "Did you read this load of crap?" The headline read: PHILANTHROPIST JENNINGS WRONGLY ACCUSED

"What?" I said in utter shock. "The man shot me!"

"Yeah. Unbelievable," Cooper said, shaking his head in disgust.

"And philanthropist? The only charity he donated to was his own!" I practically yelled, feeling heated.

"According to the article, you made up Jennings' confession. Jennings states he never told you anything about being connected to the South American drug cartel nor going after Pamela and your uncle. You dreamt up the whole thing."

"What about his Cadillac Escalade parked in my garage with the front grille smashed in?"

"It says here, it's a company car, and numerous employees have taken it."

"Yeah, so? Isn't there a sign-out sheet? Or a camera in the parking lot?"

"Guess not. But the police are suspicious because Jennings never inquired about where the company car went, and since you found it in the garage of your old home, Forensics have scraped the paint off the grille and matched it to the taxi's."

"He died," I said, and his name rolled off my tongue, "Chris Regal, the taxi driver, died from that crash." My eyes began to well. "He had a wife and daughter the same age as Savannah. Does the article say anything about that?"

"Yes. 'Jennings set up a generous fund for the widow and child' and a reward for anyone who has any information about the crash."

"Who else would know to park it in my garage, other than Jennings?"

"Dakota, I'm on your side, baby, but his defense attorneys are claiming the public knew of your life after your dad's death. You were in the media a lot. You're the youngest person in the state of Texas to receive such a large settlement from a privately owned company, and there are plenty of weirdos out there who prey on situations like yours."

"What do you mean? I don't get it. No weirdos have ever asked me for a dime."

"No. But your uncle had tried a few and won. Jake Jennings and your vacant old home were the perfect scapegoats to execute a plan to kill your uncle."

"That is ludicrous!"

"It is, but I've heard stranger cases."

"And?"

"And what?"

"Did they win?"

Cooper nodded. "They were dismissed."

And just like that, the waterworks came.

Cooper gestured me in for a hug. I stepped into his arms. He held me tightly and spoke gently, "Dakota, Jennings isn't going to get away with it. It's going to be alright. Trust me."

"I just can't believe I have to testify. I have to face him again," I cried. Cooper consoled me by rubbing my back and whispering, "Dakota, I'll protect you."

I stayed in his arms for what seemed like forever. I thought about what he had told me about his past and how he was his brother's protector, even though his brother was the older sibling. I remember meeting TJ for the first time at Rhett's bar with Gloria. She had just come to visit me and wanted to test her fake ID. I had heard Rhett's was easy to get into. Cooper was sitting beside TJ and said to us, "My brother wants to know if you two would like to join us in a game of pool?" Gloria's reply went something to the effect of, "Why can't your brother ask us himself?" and Cooper's reply, "Do you know sign language?" Gloria shook her head no but had the gall to ask, "Well, can he read lips?" I think I shrank about three feet. But Cooper answered smugly, "He's rather selective. Depends if the company is worth the effort — would you consider yourself worth the effort?" I actually let out a chuckle, and TJ did, too. The men seemed accustomed to stranger's reactions when they learned of TJ's disability. Cooper's way of acting very nonchalant about it and giving Gloria a little taste of her own medicine was well deserved and earned my approval.

TJ had been born prematurely with severe jaundice and high levels of bilirubin, which caused his deafness. He attended a specialized school for the hearing impaired for his first fourteen years. Then his parents enrolled TJ in public school but hired a sign language interpreter to shadow him. Without being asked, Cooper became TJ's bodyguard. Cooper told me horrific stories of TJ being taunted. The bullying lessened as TJ morphed into a strapping young man, became quarterback, and scored more touchdowns than any other varsity player on their high school's football team. This led to his earning a full scholarship from Texas State University. Even though TJ was older, Cooper told me he always felt like the big brother. But he also felt he had to work even harder because he had all of his five senses. He was a sophomore in high school, and TJ was a senior when their parents died.

Chapter 21

Grace

AMBER LEE had had flank steak marinating since morning, which Luke and Travis were grilling for dinner. I was drizzling balsamic and olive oil vinaigrette over the sliced tomatoes, basil, and buffalo mozzarella tray I had prepped, and Savannah and Cooper were busy making mashed potatoes while Amber Lee set the table.

Savannah twisted the pepper mill, and Cooper sprinkled the salt over the white mound of steaming potatoes. Amber Lee eyed him pitching some salt over his left shoulder. "For good luck!" he said.

She laughed. "Okay, but you've got sweep duty after supper."

He smiled. "Not a problem." Then gave a "Whoa, kiddo! That's too much," as Savannah emptied the entire bag of Parmesan cheese into the bowl.

"But cheese is yummy!"

He looked up at Amber Lee and me for approval.

I eased his worry, "We're a cheesy mashed potato family," I said, smiling.

He smiled back and slowly poured the milk in while Savannah mashed.

"Don't forget the butter," I chimed while squeezing Cooper's shoulders and planting a light peck on his cheek. "Isn't Savannah the best potato masher?"

"Yup. The best. No wonder everything tastes so darn good in this house — you three ladies know how to cook!"

I poured Cooper some wine.

"You're not joining him?" Amber Lee asked.

"Maybe a small glass with dinner, but not now," I answered. "I need some food in my stomach first."

"You are so sensible," Amber Lee said. She looked at Cooper and added approvingly, "Never have to worry about Dakota doing the wrong thing like drunk driving or flunking out of school. Honestly, Dakota, you are such a good influence for Savannah." Then realizing what she said, she quickly apologized, "Shouldn't have said anything about drunk driving — sorry, Cooper."

Another bizarre coincidence I had learned about briefly was that the young man who drove inebriated, killing Cooper's parents, was interning at the time at Uncle Travis' law firm. His name was Willet Mathews. What had happened was a terrible accident. Most of life's tragedies are accidents, followed by blame. In the onset, finger-pointing comforts the grievers in some way, as if blaming gives them something to hold onto. And when the blaming is all over and the aftermath unfolds, you have to start living again. That's just what Cooper and his brother, TJ, and their grandparents did.

"No worries," he said without batting an eye.

"Thanks, Amber Lee. But I've been foolish many times — you just don't know about them," I joked as I filled everyone's glasses on the table with cold water.

"I know I'm one very lucky man to have Dakota in my life," Cooper sweetly added just as my uncle walked in.

"Glad to hear that," Uncle Travis said, looking at Cooper, then turned to Amber Lee. "Luke needs a clean platter."

"Where's the one he brought out?" she asked.

"Outside," he answered.

"Hmm, you didn't think to bring it in so I could wash it and give it right back to you?" she said in a motherly tone.

"That'd be too logical," I teased as I reached for the platter we usually used for fish, only because it had a painted trout design on it, and handed it to him.

"Thanks," he said. "I can always count on you."

"Bring in the other one, too, when y'all return with the steak," Amber Lee called.

"Will do," he retorted without looking back as the door closed behind him.

"I bet he doesn't," Cooper snickered.

Before we ate, we all held hands. Amber Lee had us sitting boy-girl-boy-girl at our kitchen table. Savannah was sitting between Cooper and Luke. Luke and Amber Lee were at the ends. I was diagonally across from Cooper and held my brother's and my uncle's hand. My uncle and Cooper both had a hand of Amber Lee's, and she looked like she was going to burst with merriment. She recited the Lord's prayer, and after we all said, "Amen," Savannah added her own prayer, which she learned in Sunday school. It was the one she'd recited when I initially met her mother, the time Luke had me over for dinner. Janet wasn't nearly as good a cook as Amber Lee. Both women were so different. Janet was a frigid person, while Amber Lee radiated pure warmth.

Savannah sweetly delivered, "Thank you, God, for the birds that sing. Thank you, God, for the food we eat. Thank you, God, for the people we meet. Thank you, God, for everything."

"Amen," we repeated in unison.

"Savannah, where did you learn that beautiful grace?" Uncle Travis asked.

"Mrs. White from Sunday school has us say it before we have a snack," Savannah answered.

"Mrs. White sounds like a sweet woman," Uncle Travis replied.

"Yeah, and she sounds married, too," Cooper added, looking straight at my uncle.

Huh? What? Why did Cooper have to say that?

"What's that supposed to mean?" Uncle Travis asked, giving Cooper a disdainful look.

Geez, Louise! I interceded with, "Mrs. White is widowed and totally not my uncle's type."

"That's too bad," Cooper answered, taking a sip of his wine, not letting my uncle intimidate him.

"Can I have some more mashed potatoes, pease?" Savannah interrupted. Thank goodness.

"Why certainly," I answered as I plopped a heaping spoonful onto her plate next to the untouched slice of meat. "You don't like it?" I asked. She shook her head but still managed a closed-mouth smile as if to say sorry.

Luke and Amber Lee were speechless and looked uncomfortable at the negative body language my uncle was displaying. I decided to ask my uncle something I knew would totally turn his attention to me, hoping he'd let go of the wise-ass comment Cooper made, which had really surprised me. Why did Cooper care about my uncle's personal life?

"Uncle Travis, I read the column today about Jake Jennings denying his confession to me. He said that I had made the whole thing up."

"Were you surprised?" he asked, point-blank, returning to eating.

"Yes."

"Why? The man's a lying egomaniac."

"The columnist made it sound like it was true," I said, beginning to sound really annoyed both at this bullshit writer — something Tucker — and my uncle's nonchalant attitude.

"Dakota," my uncle started as he reached for the Merlot and poured himself a second glass, "Jake probably paid her."

"No! He didn't!" I was aghast. "That'd be illegal...right?" Sounding uncertain, I repeated, "Right?"

Cooper shot out a quick laugh.

We all just stared at him except for my uncle. I was inwardly screaming at Cooper, *what has gotten into you?* My uncle furrowed his brow, sliced another bite of steak, and waited to hear what Cooper had to say.

"A good columnist wouldn't do that, but your uncle's right. Veronica Tucker is notorious for taking bribes, writing garbage, and being the biggest hypocrite there is this side of the Alamo."

Taking me by surprise, my uncle concurred, "Here, here!" And lifting up his wine glass as if Cooper just made a toast, the two of them clinked their wine glasses together.

I was pleased they actually agreed on something and were back on track with being PC at the dinner table, especially for Amber Lee's sake. But I was also completely confused at their duel. And on top of that, I was fuming mad over this reporter and the lies she had written.

"I told Dakota she had nothing to worry about," Cooper said.

"Let's hope she doesn't," Uncle Travis returned. "But that's for me to worry about and take care of," he finished.

"Yeah, but don't I have to testify?" I asked, now deciding to take that glass of red, hoping it'd calm me a little.

"Yes. But all you have to do, Dakota, is tell the truth," Uncle Travis said, making it sound so easy.

"The truth shall set you free," Luke sang, sounding like a preacher as he cut a tiny bite-sized piece of his steak to feed his daughter. She opened wide like she would for a doctor — even made the "ah" sound as Luke fed her a morsel of meat.

As soon as Savannah swallowed, she said, "Mrs. White says that, too, Daddy! When somebody doesn't keen up after they make a mess, she says that."

"She wants the child to take responsibility for the mess he made," Luke explained.

Savannah nodded. "I like keening, so it's never me!"

We all laughed.

"Savannah, what does Mrs. White do if the child who made the mess doesn't come forward?" Amber Lee asked.

Savannah looked confused.

Amber Lee rephrased, "If the child doesn't say he made the mess."

"Mrs. White says, 'The truth shall set you free!'"

"That's it?" I asked

"Yup. Then Max keens it up! It's always Max!"

We all laughed again, but then Uncle Travis said, "I hope Mrs. White explained to you young minds the true meaning behind this quote." He didn't wait for Savannah to answer. He explained it to her as she stared at him in between bites of food. She nodded her head every time he asked if she understood. Then he ended his lesson by correcting her pronunciation of cleaning.

"And cleaning is with an 'l,' Savannah. Repeat after me, clea...ning," he enunciated, purposely slow, dividing the syllables.

"That's what I said." Savannah smiled. "Keening."

Uncle Travis rolled his eyes and asked rather brazenly, "Luke, when are you going to take your daughter to see a speech specialist?"

And Luke answered with just as much tenacity, "That's for me to worry about and take care of."

Good for you, bro. Sometimes my uncle can be a dick.

Travis nodded and gave an apologetic look to Luke before he turned to compliment Amber Lee.

"Amber Lee, you outdid yourself. This is one of the most delicious home-cooked meals I've had in a while."

"Thank you so much. I'm glad you enjoyed it."

"Dakota's mother, Loretta, God rest her soul, was an amazing cook, too. Her fried chicken was the best!"

"Dakota's told me." She smiled at the memory. "You're welcome here anytime, Travis. My only wish is that you'd pay us more surprise visits."

I spoke up, "I have my mother's box of recipe cards. If you want, Amber Lee, you can try to make her famous fried chicken."

"Dakota, that's so sweet of you. I would love to."

"I'll be back!" Uncle Travis said in the Terminator's voice.

We laughed.

Excitable, Savannah asked, "What's for dessert?"

"I got all the fixings for you to make your own sundae," Amber Lee answered, looking at Savannah, trying to match her animated smile.

"Yay!" Savannah cried. "Did you get choc-ate ice cream?"

"Of course, I got your favorite flavor!" Amber Lee answered.

"Hope you got strawberry," Cooper chimed in, smiling at me.

Amber Lee nodded and then directed at me, "Glad to hear he knows what you like," ending it with a wink.

Chapter 22

Black & White Photo

SURPRISINGLY, MY UNCLE volunteered to clean up.

"Someone catch me; I think I'm gonna faint!" I said theatrically, with my hand to my forehead.

"Very funny," Uncle Travis declared, playfully snapping my bottom with his coiled cloth napkin.

"All the times you ate over, you never once helped my mom with the dishes," I smirked, reassuring him I wasn't upset, nor was my mom. But it just never happened, and I wanted to know why, all of a sudden?

"Well, I am now!" he said and stuck out his tongue. "People can change, Dakota."

I laughed.

He was right. People could change. Whether it was something traumatic that altered their life or something simple that changed their point of view. Whatever it was, change for the better was inevitably a healthy move.

I volunteered to give Savannah a bath. Even though I pulled back her hair in a ponytail before she devoured her sundae, she still managed to get melted marshmallow and fudge sauce in it. I even found a few rainbow sprinkles in her gorgeous golden locks as I undid the hair elastic.

Cooper shadowed me. I was glad he didn't volunteer to help my uncle. I much preferred to keep him within arm's reach and wanted him upstairs so I could privately give him my secret gift after we put Savannah to bed.

As Amber Lee's pregnancy progressed, their staying up late gradually reduced, and they retired early. I didn't feel guilty about leaving my uncle in the kitchen alone because, for one, there wasn't really a big mess — Amber Lee and I cleaned up as we cooked, and, secondly, it made my uncle humble. My mom used to say a good man isn't afraid to do a few dishes. Sometimes my parents took longer than necessary to clean up after dinner, and when I could hear Tony Bennett, I knew the kitchen linoleum was their makeshift dance floor.

Cooper and I took turns reading aloud to Savannah from the *Amelia Bedelia* anthology, and the moment she dozed off, we both kissed her goodnight and tiptoed out of her lavender room. Once in the hallway, Cooper pulled me close to him and whispered, "So that's what we have to look forward to."

I smiled.

We heard Travis's car pull away from the driveway.

"He's gone!" Cooper said, widening his eyes. "Now I can take full advantage of you!"

I laughed and held Cooper's hand behind me as I led him into my bedroom. I teasingly pushed him onto my bed and told him, "Sit!"

He obeyed.

I went into my walk-in closet to retrieve the black and white photograph my mom had taken of me when I was four, devouring a melting strawberry ice cream cone on a hot summer day.

I reappeared, holding the nine by twelve-inch frame, and held it up for him to see.

He smiled the biggest smile. "I remember that! From your wall of photos at 1035 Triumph Way."

I couldn't believe he remembered the address of my old home in Fort Worth.

"You were so darn adorable. This one was my favorites!" Then gently taking it from my hands, he asked, "Where are you going to hang it?"

Before I could answer, he walked to a space on the wall, "Here would be perfect," he declared, grinning from ear to ear, admiring it some more.

"I'm not going to hang it there or anywhere in my room."

"All right," he said as he turned to me. "Downstairs would be good, too, so everyone can admire it!"

"No. Not in this house...in yours. It's for you, Cooper. I want you to have the picture."

He was quiet. Then he stepped closer to me and gently spoke. "Dakota, I can't accept it...it belonged to your parents...your mom took it."

"Well then," I took the framed photo from his hands and walked a few steps to the shelf across my bed and leaned it against the wall. In the same alluring manner he used with me when presenting *Winter Morning*, I finished, "You're just going to have to come into my bedroom every time you want to admire it."

He smiled.

"And I refuse to make you a duplicate — that'd be too easy."

He took me into his strong arms and kissed me passionately. We moved onto my bed and started taking off each other's clothes. Cooper got as far as taking off my top and bra before his conscience told him this wasn't right.

"I love you, baby, but I can't! Not here...as much as I want to." He groaned. "Believe me, you're killing me." And he lifted himself off of me, put his shirt back on, got up from my bed, and said, "Goodnight, baby doll. I'll let myself out."

"Goodnight," I whined, pouting, which made him come in for one last peck!

I stayed on top of my bed, half-naked, in disbelief. I knew Cooper was morally right to stop as he did. I just didn't want him to!

Chapter 23

Willet Mathews

THE NAME sounded familiar as I read another one of Veronica Tucker's columns. She had titled it THE BOY WHO HAD A FEW TOO MANY. Willet Mathews was a junior at Southern Methodist University when he interned at the prestigious law firm of Bernard Travis Kenwood seven years ago. She even had a picture of Mathews when he was twenty years old, and it was ironic how much he resembled my uncle when he was in his twenties. One of the possessions from my old house I had unpacked for my new room was an old photo of my uncle wearing a peach-colored tuxedo, with his prom date dressed in a too-tight baby blue gown. They were standing next to my dad, who was in a mint-green tux, and his prom date was dressed in a long lavender frock, hiding her figure. The colors remind me of Easter eggs, and using them for a tux should be outlawed! I took the photo off my bookshelf and examined it closer, comparing it to the newspaper photo.

In her column, Veronica Tucker referred to Willet Mathews as 'Boy Mathews' and explained how he shouldn't have been drinking to begin with because he wasn't of age. But worse was that his mentors encouraged it, pressuring him and then letting him drive off when the office party ended. Really? I inwardly fumed. How did she know? She wasn't there at the Christmas party. Tucker continued to slander my uncle, calling him a party animal and a womanizer who not only liquored up his work crew after they put in a full day but kept his private bar well-stocked for those special clients; chilled Dom Pérignon for the widows as he executed the will or represented them in their divorce.

Tucker had the audacity to refer to my uncle as 'Attorney Playboy' who conveniently had a bed in his personal office. How would Tucker know what was in my uncle's office? It's not unusual for law firms to have champagne on hand to celebrate cases won or Murphy beds in their office for those all-nighters — medical doctors have these types of beds, too! I remember as a child going with my mom to her doctor's appointment and him showing us what was behind the closed doors. He had just had it built in and was eager to show us. This asinine reporter lost all credibility when she had the nerve to blame my uncle. Mathews didn't return to the university, nor did he finish his undergrad studies elsewhere. He remained in Texas to serve his sentence: 5,000 hours of community service to be completed within five years, and attending weekly Alcoholics Anonymous meetings. Boy Mathews had to depend on his parents to chauffeur him since his driver's license was revoked for one year.

I wanted to puke! Was she for real? No mention of Mathews being responsible for his own actions. It wasn't like he was a fourteen-year-old! If he was mature enough to get an internship at a prestigious law firm, then he should have been mature enough to know when to stop drinking or admit he couldn't drive home. He probably boozed it up in college. I highly doubted it was his first time being drunk before reaching the legal drinking age, which he was only a month shy of when the tragedy occurred. Had this columnist experienced college life herself, or was she a homebody with her nose in the books twenty-four-seven? Surely, others reading this column had to feel the same way. Tucker was completely out of line, but this could be her ploy to get out-of-control write-ins. After all, bad publicity is still publicity.

And what about the real victims of the crash — Cooper's mom and dad — June and Eric Paine, who were pronounced dead before reaching the hospital? TJ and Cooper should be the ones categorized as lonely souls, having lost both parents in one night in their teenage years. Something was most definitely up with this Veronica Tucker — she was not to be trusted. She was writing a 'to-be-continued' saga, and it smelled dirty.

Chapter 24

Savannah's Fifth Birthday

NOT ONLY was it the historic "Cinco de Mayo" when Mexico won the battle of Puebla back in 1862 against the French who wanted to rule that territory, but it was my sweet niece's birthday as well, and she was turning five. Naturally, she wanted a party with her friends, but the gift she wanted most was a dog. She missed Belle terribly. Even though the first lump Luke felt on Belle's abdomen was removed, another cancerous tumor reappeared, causing her pain. She could barely walk and had difficulty breathing. With a heavy heart, Luke had Belle euthanized. She was laid to rest under one of the sweet acacia trees Luke didn't disturb when the new house was being built. She was Luke's dog before he married, and as Luke tells the story, Belle became Savannah's personal guard dog when Janet came home from the hospital with her. If Belle didn't sleep in front of the crib, she slept outside Savannah's bedroom door. It was as if Savannah were one of her own pups. As Savannah grew and tugged at Belle's fur, ears, and snout, and even climbed on her as though she were a pony to ride, Belle never minded and willingly obliged. Belle even shared her water dish with Savannah's baby doll, where she gave it a bath. Luke had captured these priceless moments on video.

Her party was to begin at noon, and the shelter opened at eight AM. Luke had called Adopt-A-Pet the night before. "Nothing like waiting 'til the last minute!" I remarked, but Luke's motto was: if it's there — it's meant to be! Fortunately for him and for Savannah, they had just received a litter of puppies from Puppies Across America. The mother was a pure-bred golden retriever, and when she was in heat, a stray had jumped the fence.

The shelter guessed the male stray was some kind of hound because they were most common in the region. They told Luke they weren't allowed to put one aside, but if he arrived right when the doors opened, his chances of getting a pup were high. So Luke and I were in the car at seven AM. Even though the shelter was only twenty miles away, he didn't want to take any chances. "We'll stop for coffee," he offered as I yawned. "Savannah's going to be so surprised."

Sure enough, there they were, all nine of them curled up next to one another, keeping each other warm. "Which one do you want?" the middle-aged volunteer asked. She wore a nametag, which read 'Lisa.' Lisa's hair was entirely gray and pulled back in a ponytail. She didn't have a spot of makeup on, not even mascara. Her slender figure was housed in baggy carpenter pants that were dusted with fur, and her worn construction boots were caked in dirt. Her T-shirt advertised the shelter. On the front, "Adopt us" was in a bubble atop a drawing of a sad-looking puppy and kitten, and on the back of the T-shirt was the phone number in bold black print: 1-800-PLZ-ADOP.

"Hey, do you sell those T-shirts?" I asked.

"Sure do, but when you adopt an animal, we give you one on the house!" Lisa answered, smiling.

Luke, reading the index card outside the pup's cage, sounded surprised, "Three hundred dollars! They aren't free anymore?"

"Nope. But the three hundred dollars you pay gets you a voucher for a free neuter or spay with any of the vets who volunteer that service. There's a list of them to choose from."

"What if we don't want to spay her?" Luke questioned.

"Then you can't adopt. At least not from here."

I gave a horrified look as I gasped, "Luke, don't blow it! Today is Savannah's birthday!" I already had the Hallmark moment painted in my mind of Savannah awaiting her surprise. Her giggles would be endless as the puppy began licking her, and she'd bellow, 'I uv you!'

The volunteer explained, "You see, there are too many strays. We can't save 'em all, but we can try like hell to prevent unwanted births. When a pup or kitty leaves us, we totally trust the new pet owner won't go back on his word and will bring the animal to the vet to sterilize it at the appropriate time. Do you promise, sir, you'll do just that?" she asked sternly, hands on hips. You couldn't blame her for being overprotective — it was part of her job, and I respected this about her.

"Yes, of course," Luke answered. "I understand."

She waited, not clearly convinced, before she unlatched the cage.

"I promise!" Luke said and even made the 'I-cross-my-heart-and-hope-to-die' sign to fully persuade this woman he was telling the truth.

She smiled. "Great! I believe you. Besides, the vets notify us after they do the procedure, so if we don't hear, we'll hunt you down!" she playfully assured him, but Luke and I both knew she was serious. "There's so much paperwork that goes along with adopting a pet," she said while opening the cage.

"How many females are in this litter?" Luke asked.

"Five," she answered as she reached in and carefully and most lovingly turned them over, looking for a girl, apologizing to them. "Excuse me, dears. Don't mean to invade your privacy."

I smiled at her winsome way with them.

"One of you lucky ladies will be going home with these nice people," she said sweetly.

Luke and I both looked at each other with big smiles.

"Why do you want a female? Just curious," she asked as she gently handed me the smallest, softest-looking, most beautiful little puppy in the world.

I met the pup's eyes and cooed, "You are just the cutest thing," as I nuzzled my nose against her teeny, tiny wet one. I was sounding like Amber Lee!

"Girls are easier," Luke answered with a grin.

The lady smiled, too. "Is that what your parents said?" Then she directed at me, "You were the easier one, right?"

I guffawed, so happy to finally meet someone who guessed right — that Luke and I were siblings! I was relieved she didn't mistake me for Luke's child he had as a teenager or his young girlfriend. Even though we had different moms, I vowed I would not put 'half' in the equation.

Then Lisa really had me when she continued with what I considered a huge compliment, "You two look alike. Your parents must have been movie stars," she crowed.

I appreciated her flattery. "Thank you. You're very sweet," I said. Then a brilliant idea popped into my head, which my mom would refer to as killing two birds with one stone: purchase T-shirts for one of the party favors while also supporting and advertising the animal shelter. Kids love T-shirts, especially ones with a puppy and kitten on them. "Do you sell these T-shirts in children's sizes?" I asked.

"Yes, of course. How many do you need?"

"Luke, how many kids is Savannah having?"

"Hmm. I'm not sure on the exact count who can make it, but she invited her friends from church and school, so that's…" He counted in his head and answered, "Eighteen. Why?"

"Because I'm going to buy some to give away to her friends," I said excitedly. "I'll take nine smalls and nine mediums. Oh, plus two adults — one for me — a small, and one for my sister-in-law — XL. She's pregnant!" I looked over at Luke. "You want one?" He shook his head. I didn't think he'd wear a T-shirt with a puppy and kitten face on it, but I thought I'd offer.

"Let me get the folder of paperwork your brother needs to fill out first. Then I'll check to see if we have that many T-shirts. Follow me." She led us to a round table with three chairs. The pup had fallen back to sleep in my arms. "What are you going to name her?" the lady asked as she pushed the middle file cabinet door closed with her butt and sat with papers in hand.

"That's for my daughter to decide. She's five today," Luke beamed.

"I've got a six-year-old granddaughter in kindergarten," she said as she marked an X by all the places Luke had to sign. "She is the apple of my eye." She then walked over to a large cardboard box and began pulling out T-shirts while looking at each label for its size.

"That does it. You cleaned me out, dear," Lisa said as she plucked the last T-shirt from the box. "Oh, the cats will love this empty box," she cooed.

"I'm done, too. I read and signed," Luke said with a ginormous smile.

"Great," she said as she quickly proofread.

"You take a check? Luke asked while taking out his checkbook from his back pocket. She gave him a once-over. "You don't strike me as the kind who'll bounce a check."

"Never. Never have, never will!" Luke declared.

She nodded. "Good!"

"How much do I owe you for the T-shirts?" I asked.

"They're eight dollars each," she said as she grabbed the calculator off her desk. "Twenty times eight. Oops. You get one free." She corrected, "Nineteen times eight is... one hundred fifty-two."

"Those are some party favors," Luke chimed in.

"Yeah, but it's for a good cause," I explained as I eased a folded wad of dollar bills from my front jean pocket, placing it down in front of Lisa and asking her if she wouldn't mind counting it since I was still cradling sleeping beauty in my other arm. Lisa looked surprised as she unfolded a one-hundred-dollar bill, twenty-dollar bills, and some tens.

Luke, also looking surprised, asked, "You always carry that much cash on you, Dakota?"

"No. Not unless it's my niece's birthday," I answered cheerfully.

Lisa returned my change, refolding the bills and placing them back in the same pocket. "Let me see if I can find a bag for your T-shirts. I know we've got some somewhere. People bring 'em in filled with old towels they no longer want. Towels make good blankets for the cages," she explained as she fished around under the counter. In mere seconds she pulled out a large bag. "This will do," she said as she noisily shook the large paper bag open by its twine handles. She threw the shirts in, giving the excuse as to why she wasn't folding them. "This ain't no Neiman's!"

I laughed.

She dropped in the stapled copies of the paperwork and addressed Luke, "The vet voucher's in the bag. Don't lose it. She'll need to get spayed at six months. That's in about four months. Okay?"

"Okay," Luke assured as he took the bag from her hand and thanked her again. "It's been a real pleasure, Lisa. Maybe someday I'll bring in my sweet Savannah for you to meet."

"Oh. I'd like that. May even put her to work — the dogs love it when someone throws a ball."

Luke touched the brim of his baseball cap in polite response, and without a backward glance, held the door open for fur baby and me as I walked out — feeling like a million bucks.

Luke and I were content on the car ride home, not talking but listening to Country Legends 97.1 KTHT. It felt incredible to hold this little fur body that would bring so much warmth into our already loving household. We were listening to Patsy Cline when Luke's cell rang, which was hooked to wireless blue tooth. It was Amber Lee. She sounded anxious.

"Tell me you got a puppy!"

"Amber Lee, wait 'til you see her. She is so beautiful," I crooned.

"Where did you tell Savannah we were?" Luke asked.

"I told Savannah you both had to finish up some pool order at the office!"

"Good. Baby, I'll be home soon — I'm at our exit now." And as Luke clicked off, he turned to me, grinning. "Savannah has no clue. This is going to be so great."

Just watching him beam, looking so proud, reminding me how grateful I was to be a part of his family.

* * *

Savannah and Amber Lee were in the kitchen when we returned home. I suggested we all sit on the floor.

Savannah cried, "Crisscross, applesauce!"

The pup began to whimper. Savannah's smile grew as I gingerly lifted my windbreaker, revealed the fur baby, and let it toddle to Savannah's already reached out hands.

"I uv her!" Savannah bellowed.

"Happy birthday, sweetheart," Luke cooed.

"What are you going to name her?" Amber Lee asked.

"Cocoa!" Savannah giggled as the puppy licked her face. "Her name is Cocoa," She reconfirmed, telling the pup, "You're my Cocoa."

Cocoa climbed — turbo charged — unable to make up her mind which part of Savannah she liked best. The moment was just as I had imagined and so much more.

Chapter 25

Mrs. Murray

"SO, HOW'D IT GO?" Cooper asked right away. "Was Savannah surprised?"

"It was awesome. She was completely surprised."

"Sorry I couldn't make it."

"That's okay. She had a ton of friends over."

"So I wasn't missed?"

"Only by me."

I could feel he was smiling.

"What'd she name it?"

"Cocoa. When can you come over to meet her?"

"I'm leaving the office now."

"Can't wait."

"See you soon. Bye."

I saw the headlights of Cooper's 4Runner turn into our drive, and I shot right out, holding Cocoa. Savannah was asleep, and Luke and Amber Lee were engrossed in a movie.

He hopped out with a big grin and kissed me first before petting Cocoa's head. "She's beautiful...and so are you." He kissed me again, holding onto my lips longer.

Cocoa whimpered, and I let her down. She peed right there, by the car's tire. I let her smell around a bit before Cooper picked her up, and we headed in.

"Would you be upset if we went back to my place? I can fix us some shrimp scampi," he asked.

"Sounds great, but I already ate." Then looking at the kitchen clock, "It is almost nine."

He nuzzled Cocoa and then looked at me with puppy eyes, too.

I smiled. "Did you happen to buy dessert? I didn't have that."

"I was planning on having you for dessert," he said seductively.

I smiled. "Time for bed," I said to Cocoa as I gingerly took her from Cooper's loving hold and walked to her small crate in the mudroom, gently placing her inside. She sniffed and curled herself in a ball as I locked it.

"Let me just go tell Luke I'm headed out. Be right back."

* * *

Cooper pulled into his reserved parking space. I carried his briefcase since he had two bags of groceries to carry in. One of them had a bouquet of flowers sticking out. When he saw that I had seen them, he said, "For my other girlfriend."

I smiled at his joke.

When we stepped into the elevator, he told me to push 6.

"But you're on 8."

"6," he repeated.

I pushed it, confused. But I didn't say anything more, wondering what he was up to.

The doors opened, and he stepped out. Then he turned to me. I was still standing in the elevator as he said, "I want her to meet you."

He wasn't joking. He had another girlfriend in the building, and the flowers were for her? What the heck?

He laughed at my bewildered state and said, "Follow me…you'll see."

We came to apartment 604, and he put down one bag so he could reach into his pockets for his keys.

What? He even had a key to her place. This was so weird.

He unlocked the door and immediately hollered, "Mrs. Murray. It's Cooper… and I brought Dakota."

"I'm in the studio," she hollered back, and I immediately felt relieved because I could tell the voice belonged to an elderly woman.

He left the grocery bags at the entrance but took the bouquet out. Then he took his briefcase from my hand and rested it near the groceries. In one hand, he held the flowers, and with the other, he held mine and said, "I want you to meet someone very special."

Her apartment layout was the same as Cooper's but reversed, and there was so much room in between the furniture — almost too much space — that it looked awkward. We headed to the second bedroom, which wasn't a bedroom, nor was it an office or a sitting room, but a bright art studio with three free-standing easels, each holding a canvas displaying a half-finished masterpiece.

"Cooper!" she said excitedly, "it's so good to see you."

"Happy birthday, Mrs. Murray!" Cooper said, matching her jovial manner while holding the flowers out to her.

She put down her paintbrush, wiped her hands on her smock, and demanded, "You get on over here and give your girlfriend a kiss!"

And he did. That was when I noticed she couldn't walk. I saw a pair of crutches leaning up against the wall behind her.

She saw that I had eyed them. "I have polio, dear," she said.

"Oh," was all I said.

Then she gave me a once-over and declared, "Cooper, your description of her doesn't fit. She's more striking than you claimed."

I released a heavy breath, as if I had just come up for air from the deep end. "Thank you." I then directed the attention away from me. "Mrs. Murray, these paintings are magnificent."

She burst out with a fun-loving laugh and said, "And a sense of humor, too? Oh, Cooper, you did good this time. Looks, brains, and wit? Don't let this one go."

"I won't," he confirmed. "But Dakota's right. Your paintings are magnificent, Mrs. Murray."

"An artist is always more self-critical, my dear." She brought the bouquet to her nose. "They smell divine."

"Would you like help putting them in a vase?" I asked.

"That'd be lovely," she answered. "I'll show you where I keep the vases, and you pick one." Then she addressed Cooper, "Cooper, dear, I'm too tired to use my crutches. Would you please go get my chair from the bedroom?"

Within seconds he wheeled in a wheelchair. Its seat cushion had one of those egg crate foam squares on top for extra comfort.

Cooper helped her into it and pushed her down the short corridor towards the kitchen as I trailed behind.

"Stop," she said mid-way, directly in front of a breakfront. "Dakota dear," she called.

"Yes," I answered as I scooted to face her.

"Open that there cabinet." She pointed to the left door. I couldn't believe the plethora of vases it held — all unique.

"This is quite a collection, Mrs. Murray," I said.

"Thank you, dear. When Richard and I traveled the world, I always made sure to purchase one from a local artist."

"Which one is your favorite?" I asked

"Oh, dear Lord, that's too difficult to answer."

We laughed.

"Each one holds a story."

I had a feeling she was going to tell me one.

"See that one?" She said, pointing, "the tallest one?"

"Yes," I answered.

It looked like blown glass in a brilliant aquamarine.

"Richard and I bought that in Greece."

"It's gorgeous," I said. "I've always wanted to visit the Greek islands."

"Oh, make sure you do. Richard and I celebrated our twenty-fifth wedding anniversary hopping from one island to the next. They were all so beautiful and the most hospitable people you'll ever meet. Delicious wines, foods. I must have gained a hundred pounds that trip!"

We laughed.

"The flowers will look lovely in it, but I can't reach it," I said.

"To the rescue!" Cooper called as he carefully lifted it up and away from the shorter vases in front that were equally divine.

I admired a scarlet vase with a mother-of-pearl inlay of a fire-breathing dragon.

"That was from our trip to Hong Kong. Richard and I bought that in Kowloon, and we were so captivated by the artist's incredible talent that we bought multiple pieces of his and gave them as Christmas presents when we returned home."

"I think hand-made art makes wonderful presents," I said.

Cooper smiled.

She took out scissors from a drawer in the kitchen, not handing them to me, but placing them near my reach. "Never pass scissors or a knife to someone you care about unless you want to sever the relationship," Mrs. Murray said in a motherly fashion.

"Yes, I know. My mother taught me that — she was superstitious, too." I said smiling, pleased Mrs. Murray already liked me. I busied myself cutting open the little nutrition packet the bouquet came with — pouring the sugar-like substance into the water and cutting each stem a quarter of an inch off at an angle before placing each flower into the vase. When I finished, she said, "Lovely. Thank you, dear."

"Is there someplace special you would like me to put them?" I asked.

"Right in the center of this table," she answered.

I placed the vase of flowers in the center of the round linoleum-topped kitchen table.

She thanked me again.

"I'm on a tight schedule, Mrs. Murray, to feed this girl and get her home before midnight," he fibbed.

"She most definitely is a Cinderella," she replied with a warm smile.

"And he most definitely is my Prince Charming," I returned with the same amiable look.

"Remember, next Thursday I'm taking you to the ballet and out to dinner for your birthday," he said, leaning in for a goodnight kiss.

"Looking forward to it, dear."

"It was lovely meeting you," I said, shaking her hand.

She returned the compliment and pulled me in for a peck on the cheek. "Good night, dear," she said.

* * *

When we entered Cooper's apartment, I put his heavy briefcase down against the end of the sofa and went into the kitchen, where he was putting away the groceries. He took out a chilled bottle of white wine.

"Dakota, I hope you aren't disappointed I didn't include you in Mrs. Murray's birthday celebration. Truth is, I bought these tickets to the ballet a year ago before we met. They're loge seats — hard to come by."

"Wow. Nice. The first time I was in box seats was when my uncle took my family to a Dallas Cowboy's game for my dad's birthday. It was awesome. That's awfully sweet of you to take Mrs. Murray, and of course

I'm not upset. I completely understand. And I'm also very impressed that you like the ballet."

"I don't really. But she adores it," he said as he pulled me into his arms. Our lips met. His hands roamed all over, from my head to my rear, pulling me in closer. I suddenly felt overheated. He was kissing me as if my breathing depended on it. I found myself unbuttoning his shirt, unbuckling his belt, unzipping him, and just when I was about to…

"In the bedroom, Dakota," he said rather sternly. "I want to make love to you on my bed — properly."

It was such a turn-on when he spoke with such assurance.

"Go," he said. "I'll be in, in a moment."

I obeyed. I didn't know if I should undress quickly and slip under the plush down comforter. I decided to sit on the edge of his king-sized platform bed — clothed — and wait for further instructions.

He entered the room. Knelt in front of me and held my face. "You won't be sorry, you'll see," he whispered as he began to undress me, starting with my Converse and working his way up slowly…very slowly. His hands gently sculpting my body. His lips followed, caressing every part…sending sensations through my body that I'd never felt before.

After we made love for the first time, which was incredible, Cooper confessed, "As much as I would love to stay in bed with you, I'm starving!"

I laughed. "Okay, cowboy — let's go eat… "It's only eleven!"

He slipped on a pair of grey sweats and a black T-shirt. "When do you have to be home?" he asked.

"Luke doesn't like me getting in much later than one," I answered, putting on my clothes.

"Then let's get started," he said as he playfully slapped my bottom. We headed to the kitchen together as I tossed my sneakers towards the front door.

I sat on the island as he served me a glass of wine and kissed me before he turned to the pot of water for his linguini and turned up the flame. Then, like a professional chef, he smashed fresh garlic cloves and threw them into a hot pan drizzled with extra virgin olive oil, and stirred it around with a wooden spatula. He added the already peeled shrimp, one hefty slice of butter, and ground pepper.

I took a whiff. "It smells so good. Do you want me to do anything, like make a salad?"

He shook his head as he sipped his wine.

"No greens?" I asked with furrowed brows.

He smiled at my motherly intentions and stepped to the freezer to take out a bag of frozen peas. He added about a cupful to the pan, lightly tossing them in the buttery sauce. "Happy now?" he teased, stepping towards me for a kiss.

"Very," I answered, and before I would let our lips touch, I whispered, "I love you." I wrapped my legs around his waist and pulled him in for a kiss.

Our intimate moment was interrupted by the sound of his cell phone ringing. Receiving a phone call late at night usually meant an emergency. His face immediately took on a pensive look. I quickly let go of my leg-lock as he quickened his steps to get it.

"Hello?" Then he went quiet, intently listening to the person on the other end. His free hand swept his hair as he said, "I'm leaving now." He hung up, letting the phone fall on the sofa as he turned to me with tears welling in his eyes. "My grandfather took a turn for the worse. He may not make it through the night." And then he fell back, letting himself collapse, the cushions capturing him. He hid his face with his hands.

I jumped off the counter and darted to him, sitting as close as I could to him. "Let me call Luke. See if I can drive you. You shouldn't drive."

He managed to say in between tears, "Driving's good. I like to drive."

I understood. My uncle says the same thing — his exact word for it is; therapeutic.

"Okay. Do you want me to go with you?" I asked.

"Yes." Then he held my hand and softly said, "I need you."

"Let me call Luke." We let go of each other as I got out my cell to phone him.

"Yes… everything's all right. Well, no, it isn't…no, we didn't get into an accident. Cooper's grandfather…may die tonight." Then I started to cry. "No. I don't want you to come get me. I'd like to go with Cooper to Dallas tonight. He's leaving soon…thank you. Yes, I'll call you when we get there, but it'll be almost three in the morning. Okay…yes, I love you, too. Bye."

Cooper returned from his bedroom, carrying a small duffle and a garment bag. I assumed there was a dark suit in it for him to wear to his grandfather's funeral, even though he hadn't died yet. But I could relate. My mom did the same thing when she found out she didn't have many weeks left. My father didn't own a suit until my mother's cancer came back at stage four. While she still could, she went out to buy what she wanted us to wear. It sounds quite morbid, but my mother faced reality head-on. "No skirting around the inevitable…if I'm going to die, I want y'all lookin' nice!" She showed us her purchases as if we were going on a vacation — a navy blue suit for Dad with a paisley tie, and a black dress for me that was adorned with baby pink roses and cream-colored squiggles. My father and I just nodded, and then she told us dinner was ready and to wash up.

Chapter 26

Cooper's Grandfather

IT WAS RATHER uncomfortable meeting Cooper's grandparents at this particular time. Still, it was such a great relief that the family acted as if they already knew me. His grandmother, Mrs. Brigham, pulled me in for a hug right away and thanked me for coming, and added, "Call me Jenny. You are so dear to my Cooper. It's so good to finally meet you." Then she led me into the room where Cooper's grandpa was — the small study off the kitchen. At that moment, TJ's wife, Linda, phoned Cooper, which held him back in the kitchen.

Mrs. Brigham spoke in a louder voice, "Walter, dear." She walked towards him and gingerly lifted his head to fluff his pillow. His eyes were closed, and I think she was trying to stir him so he might open them. "We've got Dakota with us — Cooper's dream girl. And she's even more beautiful than Cooper had described." She was smiling and then said endearingly to her husband of sixty-plus years, "Open those handsome eyes of yours and see for yourself." She then told me to sit, gesturing toward the chair on the right side of the hospital bed they had rented. His bed was positioned slightly upright. His arms were resting by his side with a tube in one of them; they seemed lifeless. She reminded him he had company and suggested I talk to him. "He can hear you," she said, looking at me with a forlorn smile. When my mother had looked like this, I remember the hospice nurse telling my dad and me the same thing about her being able to hear us. We must have sat for hours by her side and reminisced about fun times in hopes she'd crack a smile.

"Hi, Mr. Brigham, I'm Dakota...Cooper's girlfriend."

Just then, Cooper walked in.

"Hi, Grandpa! So I see you've met my girl," Cooper said, trying to sound high-spirited as he entered the room, immediately heading towards the bed. He kissed his grandfather on the forehead while smoothing back his grey hair with his hand.

I felt like crying but knew that was the last thing Cooper needed right now. So I decided to initiate a playful conversation. "Did you know I beat your grandson at pool the very first time I met him?"

Then Cooper playfully whispered near his ear, but purposely loud enough for me to hear, "I let her win, Grandpa!"

Grandpa remained motionless. I imagined his voice to be a jovial one.

"See what I have to put up with, Mr. Brigham?" I teased.

It looked as if he was trying to smile, or I was hallucinating.

Cooper volunteered, "Dakota's going to Rice in the fall."

Still silence. Walter couldn't respond, but I felt he wanted to. I started speaking. "Mr. Brigham, I want to thank you..." I was beginning to feel sweaty, and my breathing was shortened as if I had just inflated a balloon. "I want to thank you," I repeated, trying to hold back my tears, "for doing such an incredible job raising your grandson." And then I lost it, crying like I had beside my mother on her deathbed. TJ and Linda walked in as I hurried out, quickly found the powder room off the foyer, and hid. I closed the door and locked it. I did pee, but I stayed in there longer than Mother Nature required. It was so hard for me to face this again. But I wanted to be strong for Cooper. Suddenly, there was a knock on the door.

"Be right out," I mumbled, trying to calm my crying.

When I opened the door, it was Linda. She saw my teary eyes and hurried in, pushing me back inside and closing the door behind her. She hugged me. "Dakota. We know how hard this must be for you. Honestly, we don't know why Cooper brought you."

I shrugged but said nothing and took a tissue to blow my nose.

"But he did. And we're glad you're here," she back-pedaled.

"I love Cooper. This is like losing his father all over again."

"I never looked at it that way, but you're right." She eyed her watch. "I can't believe it's four AM. I am so exhausted. Lucky for us, we have this single woman, Maria, living next door who treats my kids as if they were her own."

Then she sat on the potty and peed! Explaining further, although it wasn't necessary. But I know from my own personal experience, sometimes when people are nervous or anxious, they go off on a tangent without realizing it.

"She's from Mexico and widowed. Never remarried, nor had kids. I feel sorry for her. She would have been a good mother. She's an excellent neighbor and has come to the rescue at least a dozen times. She watched Charlie when my water broke with Summer."

"My mother would call Maria a Godsend," I said as I bent my face over the sink to splash it with cool water. I blotted it dry with one of their monogrammed guest towels, trying not to ruin its neat fold.

When we re-entered the study, it was too late. He had passed. I could tell by the way Mrs. Brigham was curled up on him as I had with my mom after she went. Her head was practically buried in his chest. You want to climb onto the person you love so much and get the last of their body heat, the last of their scent, the last of their essence — their soul and touch. I fled to Cooper and held him. I felt like I was holding him up — I could feel the weight of his loss. Grief is heavy, regardless of size. I was only eighty pounds when my mother died, but I felt like the anchor of a cruise ship.

Chapter 27

The Funeral

THE URN STOOD on a four-foot-high wooden pillar with crimson roses and ivy cascading down the sides. It was a small Unitarian church. Probably could hold fifty people comfortably, but on this morning, it squeezed in at least twenty more — some mourners were left standing. The service lasted about ninety minutes, with three hymns between Mrs. Brigham and Cooper speaking, sharing what they thought made Walter Brigham special. Naturally, I was a mess. Thankfully I was sandwiched between Luke and Amber Lee, who were my bookends holding me up. Afterward, there was a catered luncheon in the Brigham's home.

About an hour into it, Cooper led me to his former childhood bedroom to ask me something.

We sat on his bed.

I couldn't help but stare at the large poster of Superman. "Real shame what happened to Christopher Reeve," I said.

"Yes. But thankfully, with his lobbying for expanded federal funding on embryonic stem cell research, 100 million dollars was approved."

I was impressed he knew this.

"I try to look at the good that comes out of the bad," he uttered next.

I was taken aback. My parents used to preach that.

"Because of him, there's a Paralysis Foundation...one that's legit. But that's not why I asked you up here." He paused and took my hand.

"Dakota, my grandmother wants to fly to Boston and scatter Grandpa's ashes in Rockport — in the ocean. Will you come?"

I was extremely touched but felt Cooper should be with his grandmother without me intruding. I held his hands and looked back into his eyes. "Cooper, I think you should be with just family."

He remained quiet.

"I only just met your grandmother and your grandfather — on his deathbed," I explained, cringing at the last part, which I shouldn't have said but couldn't help it. "I'm assuming TJ and his family are going? You don't need me. You have them."

"Dakota, I always need you."

"I need you, too, baby, but your grandma needs you all to herself. TJ has Linda and the kids. But your grandma lost her soulmate and doesn't need her single grandson's new girlfriend tagging along to such an emotional and private affair."

"My grandmother was the one who insisted you come."

I was shocked. "Really?"

Cooper nodded with teary eyes.

"Okay, I'm in." I gave him a peck and asked, "When are we going?"

"Around July fourth," he answered.

"Really?" I said, sounding surprised, trying to suppress a laugh.

"Why is that funny?"

"It's such a busy, crowded holiday. A time of celebration. With fireworks..." I paused, "You know — good times — not a time to scatter ashes."

"Oh," he returned. "Hubbell didn't come to mind?"

Now I furrowed my brow. "Why would that be funny?"

"Because you met him then, and now a year has passed, and you're with me."

"Hmm. Good point. I wonder who I'll be with next year."

"Not funny!" he retorted, pushing me back, but I could see my quip made him smile.

We lay on his bed on our backs, looking up at the ceiling, holding hands.

"Independence Day was my grandfather's favorite holiday," he began to explain. "It was always a good time spent with family and relatives who lived far away who'd make the pilgrimage to be together for this one holiday weekend. He told us that he could always count on seeing his favorite, fun-loving cousins once a year and looked forward to it when he was a boy. He promised himself when he started a family of his own, he'd carry on that tradition. And he did with my grandma, and she will continue to do so. It was what he expressed to us…his last wishes."

"Your grandfather sounds like a genuine family man."

"The best," he replied as he moved off the bed. "I'd love to remain lying next to you, but it's too tempting."

"Grandpa wouldn't approve," I teased, also getting up.

"On the contrary, Dakota. He's probably looking down at us and giving me the thumbs up."

"Very cute," I returned, straightening his tie and giving him a peck on the cheek. "Have I told you lately, I love you?"

"No, tell me again." He smiled.

"I love you."

"I love you more," he returned. "And thank you for being with me," he said with the utmost sincerity, looking into my eyes.

"I always want to be with you," I said. Before tears could well, I teased, "Now git!"

We headed downstairs and went our separate ways. I went to find my brother to let him know of my impending travel plans, and Cooper went to see how his grandmother was holding up.

Chapter 28

Returning To Rockport

THE EIGHT of us flew direct on American Airlines from Dallas to Boston on July third, but only seven tickets had to be purchased because Summer, TJ's youngest child, only just made the cut to sit on a lap. She was almost two; and adorable.

A man by the name of Sam Nelson picked us up at Logan. He was prompt and efficient. Drivers had to be, or else the state troopers would blow their whistles and gesture for drivers to move it. But this six-foot-five, twenty-seven-year-old man seemed to not care what the authorities hollered or threatened. Sure, he jumped out of his vehicle to quickly throw the baggage in the back. But when he held Mrs. Brigham's hand, time froze.

He said with the utmost sincerity, "I am so sorry for your loss, Mrs. Brigham. Mr. Brigham was an incredible person, and he will be missed."

She pushed her sunglasses up to rest on the top of her head. "Sam, thank you. He was very fond of you, too." Then she asked, changing the subject, "How's the conservatory?"

I could tell she was trying not to cry. A stranger's simple words of "Hope you are managing" or "You're in my thoughts and prayers" can set a mourner off. Or an acquaintance you run into reveals something so sweet about the person you lost that your eyes well up as fast as you can blink them away.

I remember crying at the grocery store when I eyed the cheese my mother liked. The Brie was stacked in a pretty display next to olives and loaves of French bread — my mom's favorite nosh — and I just started to

cry at the sight of it, remembering our rainy day picnic. Mom had put on a
CD, spread the blanket down on our living room floor, and we sat listening
to Edith Piaf, eating, not letting the weather dampen our spirit.

"You may be looking at Trinity's next organist!" Sam boasted as he took
Jenny's suitcase and fitted it into the trunk of his old Dodge Caravan.

"Excellent," she said, hurrying to the front passenger seat because a cop
was hollering for us to move.

Sam jumped in. "Everyone buckled in?" he asked before veering out
into the airport mayhem.

Cooper added playfully, "Ready, James!"

Sam smiled, tipping his imaginary chauffeur's cap.

An hour later, just a quarter after twelve, we were making our way
down Main Street in Rockport. I was glad Sam had turned off the AC and
automatically rolled down our windows. The smell of ocean air was so
invigorating. As Sam parked in the driveway, Jenny lightly tapped her
designer leather shopping bag-style purse that held Walter's urn and said,
"It's good to be home," as if she were talking to Walter. I caught my father
numerous times, too, talking to the air as if Mom were there.

When Sam opened Jenny's car door, he took her hand as she stepped
out of the car. He had impeccable manners.

"Oh, thank you, Sam. I do hope you plan on coming in for a cold glass
of lemonade. You know — the usual," Jenny finished with a wink.

"Only one, Mrs. Brigham. I'm driving."

"You still with that sweet, pretty music teacher?"

"Yes. Going on three years now."

"Oh good. Don't let that one get away." And then, remembering her
name, Jenny added, "Althea is lucky to have you, too, Sam."

"Thank you, Mrs. Brigham."

As he carried her suitcase into her bedroom, he lightly hollered, "Just
using the john."

I wondered what the sleeping arrangements were going to be. Where was I going to sleep? And as if Jenny read my mind, she suggested, "Cooper, why don't you give Dakota the room, and you sleep on the pullout?"

"Sure thing, Grandma."

"Oh, let me have the pullout. Cooper's bigger than me; he needs a bed," I offered.

"Isn't that sweet? Dakota's worried about Cooper's feet hanging over," Linda said and signed to her husband. TJ and everyone but Cooper laughed.

"She is sweet, and you're just jealous," Cooper teased back. "But honestly, Dakota, I prefer to be down here next to the slider than upstairs in that one-window dollhouse of a room. No offense, Grandma. I loved it when I was ten."

"None taken, dear."

"We get the bigger bedroom with two windows," Linda said, holding up two fingers, "because we come with baggage," referring to her toddlers. "They camp out on the floor at the foot of our queen-size bed. I make them nests like Mama ape in Tarzan, and they love it!"

"I bought 'em cots," Jenny reminded.

"Yes, but they'll roll off and wake us and everyone else up, crying!"

"All right, dear. Suit yourself. You know best. I don't want my grandkids waking up with a bump on their noggin, either." Jenny headed to an antique-looking table at the far end of the living room, took the urn out of the sturdy leather tote, and examined it. Then she carried it with both hands as she walked towards the slider. "Dakota, dear, will you be a doll and get the door for me?"

"Sure thing."

"And, Cooper — please make us all the usual — don't forget Sam's."

"Yes, Grandma," Cooper answered as he made his way towards the kitchen. I followed.

Cooper took out a bottle of vodka and a concentrated lemonade tube from the freezer — the kind you thawed and mixed with water in a large pitcher. But instead, Cooper used the electric blender and very little water as he degutted the tube using a soup spoon and plopped heaps into the blender, which had a chrome metal base with only two settings — on and off. It looked as if it were from the 1950s. He added the vodka, some water, and a handful of ice cubes and flipped the switch. As it churned, he set out six tall glasses. Then he turned it off and poured.

"Baby, can you reach that tray up there," he said, gesturing to a circular bamboo tray leaning against the top shelf of a corner nook.

On my tippy toes, I was able to get it as Cooper came from behind me, clasped my torso, nuzzled my neck, and fondled my breasts, whispering, "Thank you," and took the tray from my Jell-O-like arms.

He slapped the dust from it with a dish towel before placing the glasses on it. "And could you get the door, too?"

"Yes, of course, dear. Anything else you want me to do?"

"Yes, but you can't do it now."

I laughed.

Charlie and Summer were shoveling out toys from a large basket, so our path to the deck was already strewn with picture books, Matchbox cars, and wooden puzzles. We had to step around and over them to get to the slider.

Outside, Jenny lay on the wicker chaise with the urn on the side table. As Cooper held the tray, I handed her a cocktail. "Thank you, dear. Cooper, if I put together a list, would you and Dakota mind doing the food shopping?"

"We'd be glad to," I answered for us as he and I finished serving the cocktails.

"Mrs. Brigham, if there's anything I can do for you, please don't hesitate to ask," Sam offered.

"Thank you, Sam. We'll be having our annual cookout tomorrow, so I expect you and Althea to come with that delicious blueberry cobbler she always makes."

"I'll be sure to tell her. I'll pick up a tub of vanilla from Richardson's ice cream, too."

"Richardsons even have their own cows," Cooper directed at me.

"Cooper is such a good uncle — that's one of the things he does with the kids," Linda chimed in. "Summer and Charlie love the drive to Richardson's farm to pet the cows, see them being milked, and watch a video on how ice cream's made.

"So sweet," I said, smiling at Cooper. "How many guests usually come here?"

"It's open house. Some come for lunch, the beach, and the parade. Others arrive for dinner and stay for the bonfire. Overall, there are about fifty friends and relatives who show up," Jenny answered.

"When are you going to spread the ashes?" And just as I finished asking my question, I completely regretted it. I didn't mean to sound so anxious and on schedule to this very sensitive matter.

"When she's ready," Linda interjected and gave me a puzzled look.

"I was thinking of letting Walter fly over the waves in the early morning after tomorrow. That was his favorite time of day. He was an early riser and would walk to the pier and hop on with Alan and go for a ride," Jenny answered.

"Alan's the Harbor Master," Cooper interjected, "and Grandpa's summer buddy. He always went with him to make the morning rounds."

"Alan's going to take us out, so please be ready by six," Jenny insisted. "And then we'll go for breakfast at the Cobblestone Inn."

"Another pit stop of Gramps'," Cooper said, looking at me, "He always sat at the same table. Even though he let the waiter read off the specials, he always ordered banana pancakes."

I smiled. "Well, banana pancakes are the best." It sounded like Walter Brigham was popular and well-liked in this quaint town. Just then, there was a loud knock on the front door, and someone hollered, "Flower delivery."

"I'll get it," Sam said as he finished his drink and placed it on the tray. He returned with a dozen yellow roses in a clear glass vase.

"Oh, aren't they beautiful," Jenny said, admiring them, and then carefully took the tiny envelope out of the bouquet. "Well, I'll be. They're from Toad Hall book shop." She read the card out loud: "With deepest sympathy — our favorite customer will be greatly missed."

Sam was still standing with the flowers. "Where would you like me to put them, Mrs. Brigham?"

"Put them on the table here, dear, so we call all enjoy them for now. I'll put them on my nightstand later. Nothing like falling asleep and waking up to the scent of roses."

We all smiled.

"It was the only book store my grandfather would buy books from. Even back in Texas, he'd call Toad Hall for the latest James Patterson instead of going to one of the big chains. He didn't care that he had to pay for shipping," Cooper said, smiling at the memory.

What a loyal man his grandfather was, and what an adorable name for a bookshop, I thought.

"I have to go," Sam said. "See everyone tomorrow." He bent down to give Jenny a kiss on her cheek, reminding her, "Remember what I said, Mrs. Brigham; anything you need — I'm just a phone call away."

"Thank you, Sam. See you tomorrow," Jenny returned with a smile. "I'll walk you out. I've got to use the little girl's room anyway." Sam helped her up. He had exceptional manners. His parents had taught him well. My own mother would have been very impressed.

Moments later, Jenny returned with a pad of paper and pen and sat at the table. She began jotting and didn't look up until the page was full.

"There, I think that just about does it for the shopping list. If you think of anything else — get it!" she said as she ripped off the page and handed it to me.

"Did you remember marshmallows?" Linda asked.

"Yes. And Graham crackers and Hershey bars," Jenny added. "It wouldn't be Fourth of July if my great-grandchildren couldn't make their S'mores!" She was the ultimate grandmother. She tucked folded money into Cooper's breast pocket and tapped it lightly. "If it's not enough, let me know what I owe you."

"Sure thing, Grandma."

I highly doubted Cooper would.

"And we're off to the races!" he announced whimsically, kissing his grandmother goodbye, waving a quick goodbye to the rest, and grabbing hold of my hand to lead me to the infamous garage where we had made out that Memorial Day weekend when he and Gloria were still a couple, and she was showering nearby. It was such a relief their breakup was easy and amicable and that Gloria was okay with *us* as a couple now.

"Take your time," Jenny lightly hollered. "Show Dakota around."

Had she forgotten this was my second trip here with Cooper? Even though she had nurses to help with Mr. Brigham, it still took a toll on her. She had a lot on her plate, so her forgetting was understandable. I remember my dad forgetting what day of the week it was and letting me sleep in on a school day — thinking it was the weekend. That was when my mom grew very ill, and taking care of her, the household, and me were all on his shoulders. It was then that I learned to pack my own school lunches. They may have been less nutritious than what my mom would have packed, but an extra Oreo or two never killed anyone!

"Finally, I've got you alone," Cooper said as he pulled out of the driveway. "Wait till you see this place," he added.

"The grocery store?"

"The groceries can wait. I'm taking you to someplace very special first."

About a half mile later, Cooper veered off the paved road and onto dirt — a dirt road full of potholes. This bumpy road lasted a good three minutes.

"Where are you taking me?" I asked, holding on to the hanging handrail. I was practically a human bobblehead, and Cooper looked amused.

"Why? Are you nervous?" he jokingly tormented.

"Should I be?"

He took hold of my hand. "I hope you'll always feel safe with me, Dakota," he said, kissing my hand.

"Yes. I always feel safe with you," I answered, kissing his hand back. "Just not on this road!"

He laughed.

I released our hold and lightly ordered, "Two hands on the wheel, please."

He smiled and obeyed.

Moments later, we slowed to a stop. "Ah…here we are!"

There was dense forestry preventing us from driving any further. He put the Jeep Wagoneer into Park and turned off the engine but left the keys in the ignition and looked down at my feet. "Oh, good. You're wearing sneaks. Let's go check it out." He sounded like an excited kid about to embark on the craziest adventure.

I got out. He came around and held my hand. He led me through the brush and around some enormous trees until we reached a cleared plot of land with a sign that read PRIVATE PROPERTY. I had a flashback to the time Luke showed me the property he had bought to build his dream home. Was Cooper planning on doing the same?

"Let's walk further," he said, still holding my hand.

About twenty yards later, we came to a cliff overlooking the Atlantic. The view was breathtaking. "Wow!" was all I said, and then he kissed me.

We made out, but as soon as we stopped, he asked, "So what do you think? Do you like it?"

I remembered Luke had asked me the same thing. "What's not to like? It's gorgeous!" I answered.

He smiled. Then came out with it. "Dakota, I'm going to build a house right here."

"Really?" I was surprised. "I can't believe it!"

"It was the last lot. There are only five houses being built. Now I have a vacation home."

"What about your grandparents' home?"

"It fits my grandmother and TJ's family perfectly. Eventually, Charlie and Summer will need their own bedrooms, and I'm sure my brother and Linda will want their privacy, too, so the kids can have my bedroom. I can have my own house to return to after hanging with them all day."

"Yeah, but isn't that what makes it even more fun and charming — being cramped together?" I asked.

He laughed. "Yes, but it can get a little too crazy at times."

"Does your grandma know?"

"Yes. I told my grandparents a while ago."

"I'm just so surprised!"

"I was going to tell you earlier, but..."

I interrupted, "Surprised my boyfriend's this rich!"

He laughed and took me into his arms.

As we hugged, I asked, "Not that it's any of my business, Cooper, but how can you afford a vacation home — let alone a waterfront one?"

He let go, took my hands, and looked tenderly into my eyes.

"When my grandpa told TJ and me that his time on earth was expiring — that's how he worded it — he divulged he'd bought life insurance after our parents' sudden death and that TJ and I were the prime beneficiaries."

"Oh, that was really nice of him."

"He and my grandma felt bad that my parents hadn't planned ahead." He hesitated. "They actually owed more than they had, and TJ and I were left with nothing."

"Thank God you had such loving grandparents to take you in."

"Yes, thank God. And I'm sure my grandpa paid a high premium because of his age."

"So when do you break ground?"

"In August," he answered. "August first, to be exact — so the contractors say, but I know how that can go. I'm hoping everything will operate on time — according to plan."

"It will," I fibbed, remembering all the bullshit Luke had dealt with. Of course, everything came together at the end, but there were so many permits to be pulled and setbacks — some over the littlest things, too. Luke had to practically camp out, making sure the workers showed up and worked! He acted as foreman and even wore a hard hat. I couldn't imagine what Cooper would be like, especially having to deal with it over the phone instead of in-person since his business is in Texas. "I'm hungry," I said. "Let's get something to eat."

"Me, too. I know where we can get the best lobster rolls," he said, taking my hand as we made our way back to the car.

The last time I had lobster was at the Jennings' Christmas party five months before my dad was killed. That sounded so much worse than just saying my father died. I don't know why I always seemed to refer to him not being alive in such a harsh way. I suppose deep down, I was still embittered. I wish I could let it go. Maybe I was struggling with it because of the ghastly way he died. He was burned and blown apart from a pressure gauge that gave way at the oil refinery. I couldn't come to understand that it was an accident — maybe because it could have been prevented if Jake Jennings hadn't skimped on machine inspections. Why did he? So he could afford to have lobster flown in? I wish he'd skimped on the food and run a safer business instead of throwing over-the-top holiday parties. It bugged me how just the littlest recollections like lobster would set me off, and apparently, it showed on my face 'cause the next thing out of Cooper's mouth was, "What's wrong?"

"Nothing!" I lied.

"What are you thinking about?"

"Honestly?"

"No, Dakota, lie to me!"

"Jake Jennings," I blurted.

"How come? The trial isn't for a while. September, right?"

"I know. Yeah, September." I sighed. "Jake Jennings used to have a humongous lobster carved out of ice at his annual holiday party, wearing a Santa's hat surrounded by lobster tails. That's what made me think of him. I'm sorry."

"Don't be sorry, Dakota. You can always tell me what's on your mind."

"I just want it to be done and over with. Punish that son-of-a-bitch already! Jennings better not get off as lightly as Willet Mathews did," I said.

Cooper was taken aback. "Really? I thought you were sympathetic towards Willet Mathews."

"What? No! I was sympathetic towards my uncle, having to defend him — to save his career — not necessarily Mathews. Still, in the interim, he was basically set free, and my uncle didn't lose his license and go belly-up."

Cooper only nodded, looking somewhat surprised as if this was a revelation.

"Cooper, my uncle didn't kill your parents. Mathews did. And my uncle didn't pour drinks down his throat. If it wasn't after work at the office where he threw back a few too many, it would have been at a bar," I finished, feeling very flustered.

"And my grandparents would have sued the bar. The bar proprietor would have been liable."

"What if Mathews drank at home and went out — crashing into your parents' car? It would have been his fault — no one else's," I argued.

"He lived with his parents — in their home. They would have been liable."

"So your grandparents would have sued Mathews' parents?" I practically screamed. My blood was boiling!

"I don't know, Dakota. They looked at Mathews as a kid. I know he was twenty, but in their eyes, he was still a baby. What can I say? Do we have to argue about something that can never be altered?" He stopped walking, looked into my eyes, and pleaded, "Let's not do this, okay?"

"You're right. I'm sorry, Cooper. Sometimes I can't help it. It's all so fresh in my mind."

"I know. I'm sorry, too."

"One last thing, and I promise to put it aside."

He nodded.

"Why do you suppose this Veronica Tucker is so intrigued with this old news?"

"What? The gossip columnist?" he said with a look of disgust at the mere mention of her name. "How in the hell am I supposed to know that? Don't let her get under your skin, Dakota."

"Easier said than done, Cooper. But I'll try."

* * *

We pulled up to a shack. Literally a shack! A patched-up-looking shed like you'd see in a horror movie. Painted in red was a sign that read 'Mike's Lobster Shanty' with an American flag waving beside it. "Don't let the exterior fool you. It's clean on the inside. And the tables have fresh flowers on them."

"There's enough room for tables?"

"Very funny," Cooper returned. But honestly, I wasn't trying to be funny. I was serious. The place looked like it could only fit a tractor. Okay, maybe two tractors. But when we walked in, I saw how they did it. The entire back wall was blown out. There was a large flagstone patio with café-style tables covered with batik sarongs. A nice sized yard, about a quarter of an acre, abutted the patio. The lush green grass, freshly mowed, was giving off that scent I absolutely loved. It sloped down into the tiniest inlet I had ever seen — like something from a storybook, where a lobster boat named *Irene* was docked. The yard was bordered with lavender plants, lilac trees, and irises, which were also in the little vases at each table. When I looked closer, I noticed they were mini wine bottles — the single-serve ones. I bet at night, the place would be delicately illuminated. I envisioned tea lights on every table. Cooper was right. This place was quaint, and I loved the romantic ambiance it threw off. Should I ever doubt him?

"It's so romantic," I said, smiling from ear to ear. I loved being surprised with things of this nature.

"I knew you'd like it," Cooper said, pleased. "And they serve more than just lobster, in case the memory of it gave you a bad taste."

I was surprised there were only two patrons. They were sitting at one of the eight tables, sharing a bottle of wine and eating from a really tasty-looking cheese platter garnished with grapes, apricots, and figs. I decided that's what I wanted.

"Pick a table. I've gotta use the men's room."

I took a table close to a lilac bush.

A woman in her mid-forties came from around the corner. I heard a door lightly slam behind her. "Hi. You must be Dakota," she said, putting down a marble cylinder that held a bottle of white wine. She wiped her hand on her apron before shaking mine. "Pleased to meet you," she said. "I'm Melissa."

"Great place you got here," I said, returning the handshake and smile.

"Thank you. We like to call it our little slice of heaven," she said as she uncorked the bottle and filled our wine glasses halfway. "The cheese tray should be right out," she assured me with another one of her big smiles, and before I could say, "Oh, how'd you know? And thank you," she had already turned and headed to the other customers.

Cooper returned. "Hope you don't mind, but I took the liberty of ordering us wine and the cheese platter when I saw you eyeing it on the other table."

"You're amazing," was all I said.

He smiled and returned the endearment, leaning forward for a kiss.

"Excuse me. Don't mean to interrupt, but, voilà, here is your cheese plate," Melissa said, placing it down in the middle of our table. "That one's new on the menu. I made it myself," she added, pointing to one of the softer-looking cheeses.

"You make your own cheese?" I said, very impressed.

"Goat cheese rolled in herbs. The herbs are from my garden, and Mike bought me a kid. She's my favorite — doesn't give me any trouble!"

We laughed.

"Well, enjoy."

There was also Brie, smoked Gouda, and Cheddar, and I wasn't sure which one to take a stab at first. I decided to spread some Brie on a plain wafer as I asked, "Are she and Mike married?"

"Yup. Going on twenty-five years."

How many kids do they have?"

"Three — all in college."

"That must be some bill!"

"All on scholarships."

"Wow! That's awesome! How long have you known them?"

"About ten years...since the place opened. I came upon it by accident when I was biking."

"It is somewhat hidden. How do they get business?"

"Word of mouth." He looked at his watch. "In a few hours, the place will be crawling. Especially tomorrow night — you can see the fireworks from here. People bring their own blankets and spread out on the lawn. Melissa offers a variety of picnic dinners — even kid ones with toys inside — and sometimes even books."

"Like a McDonalds Happy Meal!" I joked.

"Yup, but healthier. And she places the wrapped meals in wicker baskets, not a paper bag. She gets a deposit for the basket, and the customer's reimbursed if it's returned."

"Smart, earth-friendly, and very one-of-a-kind. I like it! Do people really keep the basket?"

"I did my first time here. Still have it. Grandma keeps bread in it."

When we finished, Cooper ordered their famous rhubarb pie — the whole pie — to go, for tonight's dessert.

"They sell baked goods, too?" I said, totally wowed. "This place is amazing!"

He nodded. "They even cater. Maybe I'll use them when my house is done and we throw a party."

"Or maybe we can cook, and Melissa and Mike can come as our guests," I suggested.

"That sounds good, too. Especially the 'we' part," he said, bending over to kiss me again.

"My timing's impeccable," Melissa joked as she placed the pie box with the check on top. "Made it this morning."

"Thank you," I said as Cooper took the check, quickly examining it.

"Melissa, you forgot to charge me for the pie," he said.

"No, I didn't. There's a note inside for your grandmother, too."

My heart stopped.

Cooper stood up, and the two of them embraced. I heard her softly console him, "I'll miss your grandpa. He was the heart and soul of this community."

"Thank you, Melissa. My grandfather was very fond of you and your family, too."

* * *

Under the grim circumstances, one would think it would have been sadder, but Cooper's grandmother had succeeded in making the time a happy celebration — reflecting on Walter's life as a husband, father, grandfather, and even great-grandfather, which I think is amazing in itself. Whoever has the good fortune to have great-grandparents alive is extremely blessed. The memories Walter made among family, friends, and the community were eloquently shared. By the end of the service, there wasn't a dry eye. Walter had also insisted on a big party — not a bunch of people moping around, sitting all teary-eyed, mourning his loss. Jenny had gone along with his wishes, teasing, "You want a band, too, honey?"

About twenty years ago, Walter was the conduit behind getting a group of old-timers from Rockport Rotary who played musical instruments together to form a band. Every Fourth of July, they performed songs from the 1940s in the gazebo at the public park across Back Beach, which was just down the road from where the Brigham's summer home stood. They dedicated a song to Walter — one of his favorites, 'Sentimental Journey,' originally by Les Brown and his orchestra.

Jenny had placed the urn on an oblong table out on the deck, surrounded by an arrangement of framed pictures and a guest book to sign. The photographs depicted Walter's timeline. The one of him in his military uniform during WWII was made to look like an oil painting. Even though it was an era of turmoil, there was something almost romantic about the photograph, besides the obvious reason that all men look so handsome in uniform. Perhaps it was the glint in his eye and the pride Sergeant Brigham exuded to fight for this great country that I deeply admired.

Chapter 29

Tucker's Column

EVEN THOUGH I had a wonderful week in Rockport, it was nice to come home. I missed Savannah, and by the way she charged at me, practically knocking me down like a linebacker, I could tell she missed me, too. We sat on the foyer floor, holding one another, and we didn't get up until she told me everything she did while I was gone — from painting toenails to starting a new chapter book with Amber Lee.

"What book?" I asked excitedly.

"Charett's Web."

I knew what she meant. "Charlotte's Web was one of my favorite stories when I was a child," I shared.

"I love Wibber."

"I love Wilbur, too — it made me want a pet pig, but we got a cat instead."

She giggled. "Me, too! I want a baby pig!"

"You have Cocoa," I reminded. "And Merry."

"I rode Merry today!" she said, hugging me again.

And just then, the doorbell rang.

When I opened the door, I was face to face with Veronica Tucker. I knew what she looked like from her column — a self-portrait always went with it.

"Can I help you?" I asked rudely.

"Dakota Buchannan?" she declared obnoxiously.

"Who are you?" I asked, pretending I didn't know who she was. The last thing this woman needed was an ego boost.

She had the nerve to say, "You don't know who I am?" She didn't wait for a reply. "I'm Veronica Tucker. A reporter for the Houston Chronicle."

"Nope. Doesn't ring a bell."

"You obviously don't read."

OMG! Did she just say that? Does she expect to interview me?

"This is private property, and you're trespassing!" I practically shouted, slamming the door on her.

Within moments, Luke sauntered down the steps, freshly showered. "Dakota, you're home! Sorry I couldn't pick you up. I had a pool emergency, so I asked Hank. Were you surprised when you saw him?" he asked, coming in for a hug.

"No worries. I figured something came up. We talked horses on the drive home," I answered, hugging him back.

Hank had worked at Jennings' Petroleum doing odd, menial tasks and was what my dad called 'a slow processor,' while others called him the 'company idiot.' He was a good-looking guy with a muscular physique but couldn't carry a conversation unless it was about horses — oh, how he loved horses. After my dad died, he no longer wanted to work at the refinery, so Uncle Travis asked Luke if he could use an extra hand here at the house and the pool company. Sure enough, there was always something for Hank to do.

"Was that the doorbell I heard a minute ago?" asked Luke.

"Yes. It was that stupid gossip columnist, Veronica Tucker."

"What did she want?"

"I don't know. I didn't give her a chance."

"It probably has to do with Jennings."

"Duh!"

"Dakota, don't get smart with me."

"Sorry."

"How was your trip?"

"Under the circumstances, it was fun. Mrs. Brigham insisted that's what her husband would have wanted."

"Good. Glad she's coping."

"Where's Amber Lee? Has she been feeling all right?"

"She's showering. She's the same. Bigger, but the same."

"Still taking two-hour naps mid-day?" I asked playfully.

"Yesterday, it was three hours!"

My cell was going off. I checked who it was but didn't recognize the number. I answered it anyway, "Hello."

"Dakota, it's not wise of you to avoid me."

"Who is this?" I asked abruptly, even though I recognized the obnoxious voice as Veronica Tucker's.

"You very well know who it is. The question is, do YOU know who Willet Mathews' real father is?"

"What, as opposed to a fake father? Who cares? What does that have to do with me?"

"A lot." Then her cell clicked, signaling she was getting another call. "Think about it, Miss Buchannan," she finished, ending our conversation.

I suddenly felt a chill, wondering where she was going with this and how in the world did she get my number?

* * *

That night I offered to clean up after supper while my family took a dip in the pool. I swam every day in the ocean in Rockport and felt like giving it a rest. I rinsed out the empty milk carton Amber Lee had finished, although she never was a regular milk drinker before becoming pregnant. I discarded it in one of the recycle bins we had lined up in the mudroom. I eyed the paper bin and was debating whether or not to dig for the Houston Chronicle. I was curious to see what I might have missed while I was away for a week, and I admit Veronica Tucker got my goat. I dug all seven of them out and decided to hide in my room to read them.

Each day's column had Willet Mathews' name in the title. She was obsessed with him! Day One — *Willet Mathews' Childhood* — an only child. "So what!" I blurted. She wrote how his childhood was marred by domestic violence — an abusive father and an alcoholic mother. Day Two — *Willet Mathews Troubled Youth* — caught shoplifting and other misdemeanors Tucker disclosed. Day Three — *Willet Mathews Expelled* — caught again doing drugs. She listed all the events leading up to his expulsion from high school. Day Four — *Private School Accepts Willet Mathews* — who footed the bill? Both his parents had lost their jobs and were on the verge of losing their house. Day Five — *Happier Times before Willet Mathews* — an old photo of partygoers celebrating the New Year 1990 — all wearing paper party hats adorned with the year. An attractive young woman in her mid-twenties, sitting on some guy's lap with her arm around his shoulders. He looked much older than her — more than a decade. His hands were wrapped around her waist. Their smiling faces were boldly circled. I looked closer. Oh my God! The guy looked so much like Uncle Travis.

Day Six — *Willet Mathews Internship* — at the law office of Bernard Travis Kenwood. An old photo of my uncle when he was around the same age as Mathews was posted next to a photo of Mathews with the caption: *Almost Twins*! Then Tucker's maniacal words spewed from the page as if she had written them in blood: Was there more at risk than losing his law license — could Kenwood live with himself if his son was sent to jail for the murder of parents June and Eric Paine — and he didn't do anything to stop it? Is it highly probable that the evidence was deliberately tampered with? Day Seven — the title of this article had been heavily marred by some spilled food — looked like tomato sauce. I folded the corner of it and continued to read. Is this womanizing, blackmailing, low-life-of-a-father, a lawyer, really defending this orphaned girl, Dakota Buchannan? Or does this slime ball of a lawyer want Jake Jennings put away because he knows too much — too much about the Cardenes family, one of the biggest South American cartels and very lucrative clients of the law offices of Bernard Travis Kenwood?

"WHAT THE...?" I gasped, falling back on my pillow.

Within moments my cell rang. It was Cooper. I didn't even greet him with a hello. "You're not going to believe what I just read," I said, dismayed.

"Veronica Tucker's column?"

"How'd you know?"

"I read the same thing."

"You don't sound surprised."

"I'm not."

"How come?" I asked, beginning to feel heated. What did Cooper know?

"Dakota, your uncle's culpable."

"What?" I shouted.

"He's not as innocent as you want to believe."

"Fuck you!"

"That's nice, Dakota," Cooper shot back.

"Why do you hate him so much?"

"I don't hate him. I just...don't trust him."

Just my luck, my family brushed past my open door on their way to Savannah's room. I heard Amber Lee wish Savannah sweet dreams, and within seconds she was in my room, closing the door behind her, hurrying to my bed, and sitting beside me. I was beginning to cry. "Cooper, Amber Lee's here. I've gotta go."

"Okay. I'm sorry if I upset you."

"Me, too," was all I said before I hit End Call and looked up at Amber Lee.

She eyed the open newspapers on my bed. "Oh, you read all that stupid stuff Veronica Tucker wrote. It doesn't mean a thing, Dakota," she told me, sounding nonchalant. She even gave a wave of her hand as if she were shooing a fly. "Don't worry about it."

Oh, how I hated that phrase — Don't worry. I practically screamed, "What do you mean — it means nothing? It means *everything*!"

"Calm down, Dakota, or you'll wake Savannah."

"She's not asleep yet!"

"She's going to run in here and ask what's wrong. And what are you going to tell her?" Amber Lee was now standing by the door as if on guard. Seconds later, she returned to the foot of my bed and started collecting the papers, shaking her head and repeatedly saying, "Rubbish. All rubbish. Don't believe a word of it, Dakota." Now she was acting like the crazy one.

"Now *you* need to calm down!" I returned with sass.

Then she stopped abruptly. I was a bit taken aback by her stern stance. "You think your uncle can't be trusted if he has an illegitimate kid? This Willet Mathews boy?" She didn't wait for an answer. "You can't blame him for doing everything he had to keep his kid from spending the rest of his life behind bars. He would do the same for you, Dakota. And we don't know that he knew he had a son all these years. Maybe he didn't know until the accident. Just like your dad didn't know about Luke! It's a small world, Dakota."

"Yeah," was all I could muster.

The two of us stared blankly for a moment.

"You make a good point about my uncle. I don't think he's the type to leave a woman carrying his baby. He always preaches not to walk away from your responsibilities, and the one thing I know for certain about my uncle is that he hates hypocrisy. Even if the woman didn't want him around, my uncle still wouldn't ignore his kid."

She nodded.

"But what about my uncle's involvement with the cartel? Explain that."

"Ironically, the Cardenes dynasty does have a few legit businesses — probably to mask the ones that aren't so legit — and I'm sure your uncle's law firm was hired to draw up contracts. I wouldn't exactly say they're exclusive clients. This Veronica Tucker embellishes her articles to stir up trouble. My mother used to call people like this, shit-stirrers!"

Amber Lee made me laugh.

Folding the last of the newspapers and putting them in the crook of her arm, Amber Lee gently ordered, "Now go to bed." And with her free arm, she reached out and patted my head as she spoke lovingly, "Sweet dreams, Dakota. It'll all come together. It always does. You'll see."

"I hope you're right."

"I am."

"Goodnight."

"You'll see."

"I hope you're right."

"I am."

"Goodnight."

"Goodnight."

After she left my bedroom, my mind muddled through the list of events. How in the world was I supposed to have sweet dreams? Nightmares were more like it!

Chapter 30

Visiting With Mrs. Murray

AS I PULLED into Cooper's apartment complex, I saw Mrs. Murray being wheeled out of a van with a large blue wheelchair symbol for handicapped persons painted on the back doors. I parked and hurried over.

"Hi, Mrs. Murray…do you remember me?" The person pushing her stopped and gave me a closed-mouth smile.

"Louie," she said, "let Dakota take it from here." I was pleased she had remembered my name and smiled back.

"Okay, Mrs. Murray, whatever you say." And as I took hold of the handles, he tipped his hat and said, "Have a good night, ladies." Before we made it inside, Louie was pulling away.

"Dakota, dear, what brings you here?"

"Why Cooper, of course," I answered. It felt awkward talking to the back of her head.

"You two are back together?"

What? I didn't know we broke up. But I decided to go along — my gut told me to, and for once, I was going to follow it! "Uh-huh," I muttered.

"Oh, good. I'm glad you forgave him."

What exactly did he tell her? "What would you have done, Mrs. Murray, if you were in my shoes?"

The door to her floor opened before she could answer. "Come inside for a cup of tea, and we can talk some more. I think I even have an éclair from Spinelli's we can split — Cooper brought it for me. You do know he won't be home for at least another hour?"

"Sounds good." Cooper had given me a spare key, so I had planned on letting myself in and waiting for him to get home from work, so we could talk face-to-face about his thinking my uncle was...what was the word? Culpable?

Inside her apartment, she had me push her to her bedroom, where her crutches were leaning against a wall. "I want to walk to the kitchen from here. I've been in this wheelchair for most of the day. You go ahead and put on the kettle. I'll be there as soon as possible. I want to freshen up."

"Are you sure you don't need my help?" I asked. The look on her face said it all. "Okay," I answered as I went into the kitchen and did as I was told. I sat in one of the four chairs around the Formica table and waited. I couldn't help but glance at the open page of The Houston Chronicle to Veronica Tucker's column and quickly noticed it was titled *Poor Little Rich Girl*. What the — ?

Dakota Summer Buchannan is one of the youngest persons in the state of Texas to win a multi-million-dollar lawsuit. Sadly, her saga continues. Will she ever rid herself of Jake Jennings? Jennings' Petroleum was accused in the wrongful death of her father, Jethro Buchannan. Now Jennings is on trial for breaking and entering Dakota's home, physically assaulting her with intent to kill — firing his Glock 22 but only grazing her leg as she fled to her elderly neighbor, who knocked Jennings out with an iron skillet. It sounds almost like a cartoon. But the only thing comical is her legal counsel: attorney Bernard Travis Kenwood. Will this notorious attorney be able to put Jennings away — for the right reasons? What does this repulsive lawyer have up his sleeve? Jake Jennings is a marksman, a member of The Alpine Shooting Range for thirty years. If he'd wanted to kill Dakota, he would have! Did Jennings have a mental breakdown? Would admitting him for psychiatric treatment be justifiable?

"Dakota, dear... I got some new teas... lemon or apple spice," Mrs. Murray hollered as she came around the corner.

"Both sound good. You choose."

"Almost forgot about the éclair. Let's just make it plain — don't want the tea to take away from the chocolate!" she said as she opened the fridge to take out the small pastry box. She carried it over to the table by its string. When she plopped it down next to the opened paper, she shook her head, saying, "That Veronica Tucker — she's something else, isn't she? I don't know what Cooper saw in her."

What? Cooper dated Veronica Tucker? I wanted to scream but decided to play it cool. "Why'd they break up? I forget."

"I don't know all the particulars."

I remained quiet, hoping she'd divulge some details.

"I saw her here not too long ago, so they still keep in touch. I don't blame you for being mad at him for that."

So that's how she called me on my cell. Cooper gave her my number. I was fuming mad but remained speechless.

"Dakota, don't worry, though. It's you he truly loves."

Argh! Don't worry!

The kettle whistled. I quickly got up, removed it from the stove, turned off the burner, and poured the hot water into the teapot. I put a Lipton tea bag in before closing the lid.

"There are clean teacups in the dishwasher," Mrs. Murray said.

"Let me help you empty it," I offered, removing two teacups from it.

"Don't bother, dear. When you live alone, it's easier this way."

I noticed a small stack of dirty plates in the corner of the kitchen sink — she had a system. I was dying to learn more about the shit-stirrer's relationship with my Cooper, but something triggered Mrs. Murray to tell me about her late husband. I listened patiently.

"Richard died of a heart attack last year — about the same time Cooper moved in. News spreads — 'Did you hear about that poor, crippled widow in 6C?' was the gossip. Don't get me wrong, dear, I knew they meant well. Everyone was nice, bringing me food — meals and casseroles, but Cooper was the only one who offered to take me out to dinner. Thought it'd do me good to get out of the house, so I could pick what I wanted to eat. Good thing, too, because I was getting so sick and tired of lasagna. Why does everyone always make lasagna to bring over when someone dies?" she asked with a dismayed look.

I chuckled. It was true. "When my mother died, people brought over lasagna, too — our freezer was stacked to the brim with them. Easy to make, I guess," was my answer. "And it's better the next day and the next!" I kidded.

She agreed, "I suppose — that's if you can stomach the same thing over and over again. I was never one for leftovers. Anyway, Cooper didn't seem nervous about how he would get me in and out of his big car. He was so patient with me. Even asked if I wanted to go to a jazz club afterward!" She laughed. "But I think he was just teasing."

"You should have called his bluff."

"What?" Mrs. Murray said, completely befuddled.

"You should have said okay. Okay to the jazz club." I smirked while inwardly screaming — I couldn't believe he never told me he dated Veronica Tucker and then gave her my number! What kind of boyfriend was he? Did he love her? Does he still?

"Oh, Dakota. Don't be silly. I'm much too old to be clubbing!" She smiled but then gave her shoulders a little shimmy, adding, "although, that would've been fun!"

I smiled. Mrs. Murray was a pistol.

"Instead, I told Cooper to take me to the grocery store. We filled a whole basket full. We talked and talked as I steered myself down each aisle. You know, in one of those little electric buggies with a big basket in the front. It was so much fun. I really wasn't paying much attention to what I was throwing in. I just loved hearing him talk. He reminded me of Richard."

I tried to look happy for her sake, but she saw right through it. Cupping her tea as if heating her hands with it, she admonished, "Dakota, dear, don't be mad at Cooper. I'm sure he had a good reason."

I wanted to argue, but instead, I just shrugged my shoulders. I tried to blink away my tears. Mrs. Murray grabbed the tissue box and placed it in front of me.

I sniffled and blew my nose.

"Knock, knock," a voice called. I knew right away who it was.

"Cooper, dear…we're in the kitchen," Mrs. Murray hollered.

He came around the corner. "I thought that was your car I saw parked outside," Cooper said, all smiley as if everything was hunky-dory. But then he saw my reddish complexion and froze. "Dakota, what's wrong? Were you crying?"

"Is Veronica with you?" I blurted.

"What?"

"Mrs. Murray told me."

Now she looked puzzled.

"I see," was all he said.

Mrs. Murray responded, "Oh dear, I stuck my nose in where I shouldn't have."

I immediately felt terrible for tricking her. "It's my fault," I said. "I led you to believe I knew what you were talking about."

Cooper just stood silent.

Then Mrs. Murray gave him a stern stare. "Cooper, why weren't you honest? Dakota had a right to know."

"Mrs. Murray, with all due respect, I don't think a current girlfriend needs to be privy to past ones. I didn't question Dakota on her past lovers."

I was fuming. He knew I lost my virginity to Hubbell.

"You both are young'uns — stricken with more grief than what most people experience in a lifetime. Don't play games with one another." She then quickly excused herself, and as fast as she could walk in her crutches, she left the kitchen and hollered, "I'll be in my studio."

As soon as I heard the door shut to her studio, I stood up to leave.

Cooper quickly grabbed hold of my waist, pulling me in, causing me to fall back onto him. He stood firm, holding me, and sighed, "You won't understand."

I elbowed him to let go, desperately trying not to cave.

He didn't let go. Instead, he turned me around, looked tenderly into my eyes, and pleaded, "Please let me at least try to explain."

"Half-truths are another form of lying," I told him.

He looked guilty but had the gall to say, "I didn't lie. I just didn't tell."

"Do you really believe that not telling is not lying?"

He licked his lips and said nothing.

"You made it sound like you only knew Veronica Tucker through reading her column," I continued, not relenting.

"You want the truth?"

I remained firm, not giving into the soulful look he was giving me, and gave him a smart-aleck retort, "No, Cooper, lie to me."

"I'm actually embarrassed I went out with her."

"So why did you?"

"Okay, since you want honesty, I'll tell you." He let go of my waist, combed his hands through his hair, looked up at the ceiling as if asking God for strength, and blurted out, "It was a one-night stand."

"Hmm, usually one-night stands mean one night!"

"We were drunk, and I didn't know who she was at the time."

I waited. "And?"

"I left her place with a killer hangover."

He looked at me like I should feel sorry he suffered a killer hangover. "Go on," I said sternly.

"I snuck out, Dakota, while she remained sleeping, and she tracked me down!"

I suppressed a laugh. He really looked pathetic. I remained firm, "So?"

"So?" he returned. His voice rose, "She wouldn't take no for an answer!"

I gave a snide laugh this time. "So you're telling me she forced you to take her out on a legit date!"

"Yes!"

"Oh, poor baby. And the sex wasn't good?"

"Dakota, I have a reputation."

I laughed. "What?" I couldn't believe he'd just said that. "A reputation for being good in bed? Please. Don't you think you're being a bit narcissistic, Cooper?"

He laughed, "I kinda like this tough Dakota I'm seeing right now."

"Don't, Cooper. You're making it worse."

"Dakota, if you haven't noticed already, I am a gentleman. That's the reputation I'm referring to."

"Except for that one night?" I questioned.

"Yes. Shots of tequila got the best of me."

"Where'd you take her on this date?"

"We went to a casual restaurant, and that's when I told her that it was a mistake we slept together."

"How'd she take it?"

"Calmly, and then suggested we get to know each other. I told her I wasn't interested, and then she assumed I must be gay!"

I laughed.

"So, I think she's very jealous of you."

I laughed. "Is that supposed to make me feel better?"

He laughed and asked, "Does it?" tugging at my belt loop. And before he let me answer, he kissed me.

"Not so fast! Mrs. Murray told me she saw Veronica Tucker here only a short while ago."

"She heard about my grandfather and came over to see how I was doing and asked if there was anything she could do."

"And you said?"

"Oh, Dakota, I said what any person would say, 'thank you,' and then bragged about you and told her she should leave. She asked to use my cell phone because hers was dead. I told her sure and went to the bathroom. When I came out, she was gone."

"So that's how she got my number! That bitch!"

"What?"

"Yeah, Veronica Fucker called my cell and threatened me not to ignore her!"

"I admit when she found out that I was the one who donated blood for your uncle's operation — the uncle who defended the shithead who killed my parents — she couldn't believe it. She must have said to me, 'What a small world it is' at least a hundred times."

I stood speechless. Fucker was right. What were the chances?

"Wait a minute. You thought I gave her your phone number?" Now he sounded angry with me.

I looked down.

"Dakota." Then he eased up. "So am I forgiven?" he asked.

I looked into his eyes. "You can honestly admit to me that there is nothing more going on between you and her — other than her filling your head about how crooked she thinks my uncle is?"

He acted it out as he replied, "I cross my heart and hope to die." Then he gently brushed my hair away from my face, cupped my cheeks, and said,

"Dakota, it's you I love. You're the first girl I have ever fallen this madly in love with...and would do anything for."

"Anything?"

He gave a sultry smile and repeated, "Anything."

"Will you get her to stop?"

He let go of my face. His sexy look turned stern as he defended, "Dakota, she's just doing her job. So, no, I won't ask her to stop."

"Even though they're lies," I said.

"Even though they're lies," he returned. And just at that moment, the door buzzer rang. Within seconds Mrs. Murray was hollering, "I ordered Chinese — enough for the three of us. Let's open a bottle of wine, too!" as if this was a celebration. "I could go for some Merlot with my Moo Shi!"

She was quite adorable, and Cooper and I laughed. "Oh good," she said, coming around the bend to grab her coin purse from the junk drawer. "I knew you'd kiss and make up." She took bills from the sequined purse and then went to answer the door. Within moments she was leading a short, middle-aged Asian man wearing a white apron into the kitchen.

I inwardly laughed at this very stereotypical appearance, and then when Mrs. Murray added, "Ping, dear, put it right down on the table," I chuckled and quickly said, "Hello" to make up for it.

He nodded hello to Cooper and me and asked, "Anything else, Miss M?"

"No, dear, but thank you," she answered as she put the folded bills into one of his hands and repeated her thanks.

He was thankful, nodded a good-bye to Cooper and me, and left.

She pointed to a cabinet with one of her crutches. "Dakota, dear, in there."

I opened the cabinet — it was heavily stocked with wine. Mrs. Murray saw my surprised look and offered, "What can I say? I like wine!"

"Which one?" I asked.

"Surprise me. I like 'em all."

I picked one from Israel.

"Dakota, do you know how to play gin rummy?" Of course, I did, but even if I said no, something told me she'd teach me. I knew this was going to be a long night, but it was just what I needed. As much as I wanted to make love to Cooper, I knew having him wait would be a suitable punishment.

I also regarded what my parents told me, which was how it was important to respect your elders and pay close attention, particularly to the lonely ones. "Someday, you'll be old and will want company, too," my mother often reminded me as I tagged along, running errands with her for some of the elderly residents at the independent living facility where my mom volunteered. Sometimes when Mom picked me up from school, she'd say how we had to shoot over to the home and do a quick drop-off. But even after delivering their medicine prescriptions, we always ended up staying to help with something else, like fixing the television — an accidental push on the remote control sent the program off and the old person into a frenzy! I often was asked to crawl under a bed to reach for some thingamabob they had dropped. They always rewarded me with candy. But first, I had to open the bag of peppermints or butterscotch hard candies because the old person said she was "all thumbs!" The elders would ask me to recall my day at school just so they could relive theirs — back in 1930! I have to admit, some of their stories were fascinating, making my generation look very lazy in comparison. Talking with Mrs. Murray reminded me of those times with Mom at the old age home, which made me smile. Now that I knew she was a busybody like my old neighbor, Mrs. Turner, I inwardly laughed. Another thing Cooper and I had in common: nosey old lady neighbors who meant well.

Chapter 31

The Suicide

I HAD PHONED Luke to let him know I was going to stay over at Cooper's. He seemed all right with it. I mentioned hanging with Cooper's elderly neighbor, who was kicking my derriere in gin rummy between eating Chinese take-out. I left out the part about downing a bottle of red. "Sounds like fun!" were his exact words, and he suggested we ought to do that one night.

* * *

I awoke to the delicious smell of brewed coffee and moseyed to the bathroom. Upon my return, I was pleasantly surprised. Cooper was back in bed, modeled perfectly, holding two mugs of coffee. I smiled but suddenly felt shy standing there naked and began to blush. "Come here," he said as he carefully put down the mugs on the adjacent nightstand. He playfully grabbed me and hid me under the covers, capturing me for another romp. I could spend all day with him in bed, swallowed in his arms.

Thankfully, the knock came after we were finished. It was Mrs. Murray. She sounded overly excited, like she had just won the lottery. Cooper quickly opened the door. Mrs. Murray stood, her crutches holding her up, and in her hands was the Houston Chronicle. The headline read: JAKE JENNINGS KILLS HIMSELF. I gasped and stumbled back. Cooper caught me as Mrs. Murray hurried in and closed the door with the butt of one of her crutches. She continued to holler, "Dakota, he was guilty! No one kills themselves unless they are hiding something, and they can't live with the deceit." She threw the paper down on the coffee table and gave a heavy sigh. Cooper pulled up a chair for her to sit.

I dropped myself onto the sofa, hid my face in my hands, and cried, trying to take it all in. Although this was tragic news, it was also good news. "Dakota, it's all over. You won't need to testify," Cooper said softly as he sat down next to me and smoothed back my hair. I reached for the paper, and as I scanned the article, searching for details, I wondered if this was really a suicide or if someone pushed him off his balcony. For some really weird reason, I felt unsure.

***

When I walked into the house, Amber Lee immediately hugged me. "I told you things always have a way of working out," she said.

I was surprised at this — she thought Jennings killing himself was considered 'worked out.' It actually made me more suspicious.

"Now, you don't have to testify. You can start college with a clean slate," she finished.

I admit I was relieved that there'd be no trial to pull me away from classes.

"Yeah," I answered, feeling fazed. "My mom used to say, 'look for the good in the bad.'"

"Your mother was a wise woman."

Just then, Luke came down the stairs, wearing a paint-covered smock. "We need paper towels, pronto!" Then he saw me, "Oh hey, Dakota." He couldn't pass his wife without planting a kiss on her. "Did you hear what happened to Jake Jennings?" he directed at me.

"I'd be pretty stupid if I hadn't."

"A simple yes would do," he said sternly.

I apologized, "Sorry, Luke. I'm just shocked by it. Never pegged him for someone who'd take his own life. He seemed so full of himself — not depressed in the least."

"Yeah, me too. But this is quite a relief for you," he replied.

"Of course," I answered, taking an Oreo out of the cookie jar. I twisted it apart, scraping the white filling with my teeth. "I'm anxious to read his suicide note."

"Note?" Luke asked.

"Yeah, note. A suicidal person usually writes one before killing himself, you know, to say why he chose to take his life and maybe confess what he did wrong if he's feeling remorseful."

Both Amber Lee and Luke were staring at me, looking completely clueless.

"Oh my God. I can't believe you don't know this! All movies with a suicide show a letter at the crime scene. Everyone knows that, duh!"

"This whole time, Amber Lee, we've been watching the wrong movies," Luke chided.

"You better go see what Savannah's up to before she paints a wall," I warned. Luke kissed Amber Lee again and fled up the steps with the entire roll of paper towels.

"The Chronicle didn't mention a suicide note," Amber Lee said, "but they probably can't reveal it just yet."

"Yeah," I agreed.

"How's Cooper?"

"Dreamy," I said, all smiley. And just then the phone rang. Caller ID read Gold. "It's Gloria," I told Amber Lee.

"Oh, good. Tell her I say hi. I'm headed upstairs to see what Monet and Picasso painted!"

"Hi, Gloria!"

"Dakota, you're not going to believe this." She didn't let me guess. "Pierre invited me to spend Christmas with him in Paris!"

"I thought he was Jewish."

"He is. But you know what I mean. Winter break — four weeks in Paris! And he's buying my plane ticket. He told my parents that was the least he could do. Dakota, he is sooo hot," she embellished. "Better than Cooper. No offense."

"None taken," I said. Honestly, I was relieved she was able to get over Cooper so quickly.

"How is Cooper?" she asked, but I knew it was bogus. She didn't really care how he was — she was too excited about Pierre and sounded anxious to turn the conversation back to herself.

"Awesome," I answered. Then asked, "Is Pierre in college?"

"In France, they call it university," she corrected. "And yes, he's attending the Sorbonne — where you want to study abroad, right?" And before I could answer, she teased, "Better not steal him, too."

I was stung.

"I hope you're joking," I said. I knew I didn't steal Cooper. He pursued me.

"No, I'm not." She waited for a brief second before she cheekily chimed, "Pierre does attend the Sorbonne."

"Very funny." I quickly changed the subject. "Did you hear what Jake Jennings did?"

"Kissed the ground from a thousand feet," she answered. "That's my real reason for calling, but I didn't want to start off with that."

"Thanks," I said, amused with how easily Gloria could make light of a serious situation.

"You must be relieved," she asked.

"Very. But also curious about his suicide note."

"Your Uncle Travis can find out for you. That is, if he isn't too busy playing catch-up with his son — you know, to make up for lost time," she joked.

"You're just a little comedian," I returned.

"Don't get me wrong, Dakota. I love your uncle. And I don't think Veronica Tucker has it all down. There's more than meets the eye, as my Bubbe would say. There's a lot this so-called reporter is leaving out."

"I agree."

I wanted to divulge about Cooper and Veronica but decided this was not the right time. I imagined Gloria would flip out. Instead, I stayed on topic. "If my uncle knew he had a kid, he'd want to be a good dad."

"Look how he treats you. You're like a daughter to him. He may be a ruthless lawyer, but when it comes to you, he's a papa bear protecting his cub!"

"Exactly," I agreed.

"And Dakota, your uncle does have scruples. Don't believe everything that reporter wrote."

"Hey, am I going to see you before you head to Yale? I can ask Luke and Amber Lee if Pierre can come. You can show him Houston. Amber Lee loves meeting new people. She'd have a field day with a Frenchman — probably make some French dish one night! Of course, he'd have to stay in the guest room, and you would have to stay with me in my bedroom. No funny business, or Luke would have a coronary."

"I'd love to. Pierre may be wildly passionate, but he is very proper and respectful when it comes to parents. Besides, it would make it more exciting for us. This will be so great. Thanks, Dakota. I can't wait! That is, of course, if my parents say yes."

"Let's hope Luke says yes, too. And there's no doubt in my mind you and Pierre will find a way. Just don't sneak out and come back after midnight!" I said, remembering the night of my uncle's car accident when Gloria stayed with me but wasn't home at the curfew Luke gave her. She was out with Cooper.

"I promise to behave," Gloria agreed. "Okay, gotta go convince the folks. Bye!"

I laughed, envisioning her hurriedly finding her parents and pleading for permission. "Bye," I said, hanging up.

I stayed put before letting Luke and Amber Lee know what I had just proposed. I sat on the kitchen stool, wondering how Gloria and Cooper would act. I always thought it was strange to be friends with past lovers, but some people don't think it's warped. I was hoping they'd be two of those people. I wondered how it would be now that it was discovered my uncle had an illegitimate son — and how ironic it was that he's the boy who accidentally killed Cooper's parents. I wondered how Savannah would be with me being away at college and her at home, playing big sister. I smiled, feeling confident that she would be the doting kind of sibling rather than jealous — being mean just wasn't in her nature. There were a lot of changes coming our way — all good — and most definitely, they would play an intricate part in all our lives. I considered us a close family. No matter what, we would overcome any obstacles we stumbled upon and make the best of what God served us.

Chapter 32

A Parisian Dinner

I WAS RIGHT — Amber Lee got out her French cookbook and began searching for recipes to prepare a French culinary delight for our foreign visitor. They were only staying for two nights, but Amber Lee's intent was a three-course dinner on the first evening. Luke convinced her that the second night Pierre ought to get a taste of Texan BBQ, although I'm sure he had that with the Golds. Excitedly Luke proclaimed, "We've gotta take Pierre to Rhonda's Rodeo Roadhouse. He has to ride the mechanical bull and line dance before he heads back!"

"Okay. I suppose you're right. That'd make a good story for him to tell back home," Amber Lee said, smiling at her boyish husband. "Didn't know you loved that place so much."

I was psyched to see Gloria again before she headed to Connecticut for college. I was relieved that Cooper would be out of town on business, and I knew it was legit. He told me before I had told him about Gloria and her Frenchman's visit. It was some annual advertising convention he always attended. I knew that eventually I would have to deal with Cooper and Gloria's first encounter since their breakup, but I didn't feel like dealing with it just yet. And when I told Gloria that Cooper was going to be out of town, she sounded relieved, too, and told me Pierre knew nothing about it. As if it were scandalous!

Savannah, Luke, and I were out riding when Gloria and Pierre arrived a little earlier than planned. We heard Amber Lee laughing on the veranda and knew Gloria was telling one of her stories. As soon as we showed, Pierre stood up and came over to shake Luke's hand. Then he kissed me on each cheek while holding my hand. I wasn't surprised. His greeting is typical of Europeans.

Gloria shuffled over to Savannah and quickly captured her in a high hug, squeezing her and telling her how much she missed her.

Naturally, Savannah giggled and put her hand out, bellowing, "I'm five!"

"What a big girl you are!" Gloria replied, tickling Savannah under the arm. "I think there's a gift in my bag with your name on it!" pointing to her duffle resting on a nearby table.

Savannah smiled, and as soon as Gloria put her down, she playfully swatted Savannah's bottom with a "Git!"

Pierre spoke English very well but with a strong French accent. Amber Lee was already smitten with his looks and demeanor. He was about six feet tall, slender, with wavy blond hair, blue eyes, and an alluring smile that showed off his perfectly aligned teeth. She even asked if he ever had braces, and when he said no, she said, "Wow, your teeth are perfectly straight!" I caught Luke rolling his eyes as he helped himself to a beer.

"Luke, where are your manners? Pierre, would you like a cold beer?" Amber Lee asked.

"No, thank you. I don't drink beer. But can I get you something?" Pierre asked, not taking his eyes off of Amber Lee.

"That is so sweet of you. I'm fine, thank you." She lightly rattled the ice cubes in her glass. "I still have some of this delicious iced tea...but merci beaucoup!" she said, all cutesy-like, impressed with herself for speaking French.

"Hon, is it tonight you're making that French dinner or tomorrow night?" Luke asked, sitting down across from her.

She answered but directed it to our French guest, "Pierre, I'm sure I can't come close to your mother's cooking, but I have had chicken marinating all day for coq au vin."

"Ah yes, one of my favorites. And you will probably surpass my mother, for she is not a cook. She paints beautifully, though. My father is the cook."

"So tonight we stay home, and tomorrow night it's Rhonda's?" Luke declared, but in a questionable tone as if he wanted Amber Lee's final approval.

"Yes, honey. Now, could you show our guest to his bedroom? I'm sure he wants to freshen up."

"Is there time for a swim?" Gloria asked. "I would love it after the long car ride."

"Of course. Dinner won't be for another two hours," Amber Lee answered, then enthusiastically asked, "Pierre, do you like to swim? You look like a swimmer!"

I spied Luke rolling his eyes again, looking both surprised and bothered at his wife's flirting. I couldn't help but guffaw and patted Luke on the chest, saying, "It'll be okay, buddy." Amber Lee looked as though she was dying to see Pierre in a swimsuit. It had to be all those hormones swishing through her body making her giddy. I had read an article in Cosmo magazine about how pregnancy made women hornier.

"Yes. I am on the swim team at the university." He smiled as Luke led him away, making Pierre carry his own duffle bag.

I hoped the suit he brought wasn't one of those Speedo types most European men wear.

And just when they were out of earshot, Gloria quietly said, "Don't worry, he brought trunks," as if she read my mind! The two of us laughed as we trailed behind.

While Luke was helping Amber Lee with dinner, the four of us were in the pool, splashing about, tossing Savannah as she pleaded, "More…more,

...again...again!" Already Savannah had made her way into Pierre's heart. The time sped by because, before we knew it, Luke was giving us a thirty-minute warning — enough time to shower and change before dinner was served. This wasn't the type of dinner where we could show up with a towel wrapped around us or a cover-up. Besides eating in the formal dining room, Amber Lee had gone all out with linen napkins, fine china, and she even polished the sterling silver flatware that her great aunt bequeathed to her on her wedding day. So the least I could do was wear something nice and tell Gloria to do the same, although she didn't need much coaxing. Gloria loved clothes, and she took any chance she could to interchange them throughout the day. Someday, she'll make Hollywood proud. That's if she still wants to become a movie star.

* * *

"Magnificent," Pierre declared. "This has to be the most exquisite table setting I have ever laid eyes on. And the aroma..." he breathed in. "Divine."

"Really?" Amber Lee said, looking flustered. "Thank you, Pierre."

Pierre smiled.

"Yes, honey, really. You're amazing," Luke said and blew her a kiss which she caught in mid-air and placed on her cheek. She immediately gave an exaggerated sigh, batted her eyelashes, and smiled, acting like a fairytale princess. We all laughed at her goofiness. We sat down, except for Luke, who had begun pouring the already open bottle of Burgundy. Pierre immediately put a flat hand over the rim of his glass and said he was happy with water. What kind of Frenchman doesn't drink wine?

Amber Lee led grace.

"When will the baby be here?" Pierre asked, slicing his chicken.

"Mid-October," Amber Lee answered excitedly. "Same month as Dakota's birthday!"

"Have you thought of names?" Pierre asked.

"If it's a girl, I think Desiree would be a nice name — don't you?" she directed to Pierre.

"You never told me that," Luke said, slightly offended.

"Just thought of it — really," Amber Lee answered.

"From desire," Pierre said, nodding approvingly with raised eyebrows and a slightly mischievous grin as he repeated, "Desiree. Yes, very good name…very sexy."

Amber Lee was in awe and blushing. Gloria was oblivious — she was busy mimicking Savannah, who had turned her cloth napkin into a babushka's scarf, and the two of them were making funny faces at each other, in their own little world. And Luke? Well, he looked as if he wanted to throw his knife at this brazen Frenchman! Like a dad wants to hear his daughter's name is sexy! Pierre was such an idiot — had he forgotten we were talking baby names, not cabaret?

"And if the baby's a boy?" Pierre asked, still staring at Amber Lee with an alluring look.

"Oh, that's easy. He'll be named after my dad…Jethro Theodore Buchannan," Luke interrupted abruptly.

"But we're going to call him 'Teddy' for short," Amber Lee interjected.

"I didn't know that!" I said, pleasantly surprised. "Teddy Lockwood does have a nice ring to it. Dad would have been thrilled at this, Luke."

Luke immediately beamed and said, "Thanks, Dakota. That means a lot to me."

Gloria, still with her cloth napkin over her head, not tied at the neck only because it was too small, chimed in, "In the Jewish tradition, you name after the dead. Not that this means anything to you — just thought I'd throw it out there!"

My friend looked goofy and adorable. I was impressed that she could listen to the adult conversation while paying attention to Savannah. Then she added cheekily, "Always good to teach my Lukey about my culture!"

Amber Lee and I laughed.

"Very funny," Luke returned.

Pierre looked quizzical, so Gloria turned to him and explained — still with the napkin atop her head. "Luke had never heard of challah — not even challah French toast!" as if this was the end-all.

Pierre was quick to comment, and he had some nerve to swipe the napkin off her head. Tossing it down on the table beside her plate, he declared, "There is no such thing. French toast is made with a baguette that you soak overnight in egg, milk, cinnamon, and come morning, you bake it. When it comes out of the oven, you pour melted butter and warm maple syrup on it, toss fresh berries atop, sprinkle with confectionary sugar, and serve. This is delicious. This is how my father makes it. That is real French toast. The other must be American."

Gloria just stared at him. She was fixated on his mouth, and a sly smile started to form on hers as if she thought he sounded sexy. I actually thought he sounded snobby and pretentious. And who asked him for the recipe anyway? I couldn't help but laugh when I saw Luke opening another bottle of wine, shaking his head as he pried the cork free. I imagined the bubble over his head read, "Remind me never to take Amber Lee to Paris!"

I was proud Gloria didn't give in and apologize to Pierre. I was hoping she'd declare that challah is the only way to make French toast! Instead, she collected her cloth napkin and returned to acting silly with Savannah, which I appreciated even more.

"Will you teach me to make it tonight so we can have it for breakfast in the morning?" Amber Lee asked and then added as if she was a schoolgirl, "I'm a very good student."

Didn't she pay any attention to his reciting the recipe? Doesn't take a brain surgeon to remember it.

Pierre smiled back. "Of course. It would be my pleasure. That is the least I can do. You are very kind to have me stay here."

I felt I should warn him to sleep with one eye open but then decided he wouldn't understand the joke. He was fun playing in the pool with Savannah, but at the dinner table, he seemed pompous. I was glad he didn't drink because he probably would have snubbed the bottle Luke had paired with dinner and give us an unsolicited lesson on wine. I hoped he'd loosen up tomorrow at Rhonda's. Then I smiled, knowing Amber Lee had requested Betsy's section. If there was anyone who could set someone straight, it was brazen Betsy. He wouldn't know what hit him. I inwardly smiled, picturing him on the mechanical bull, and thought I just might have to capture it on video to put on YouTube!

Chapter 33

Wild Turkey

I LITERALLY SCREAMED. Screamed with joy when I saw my uncle head straight to our table. I pushed back my chair and stood up, and as soon as I turned, I was captured in his great big loving arms. In the excitement, his Stetson toppled off onto the chair. "Oh, Dakota, I'm so sorry," Uncle Travis uttered.

"I'm sorry. I'm sorry I didn't call you. I'm sorry for thinking badly about you," I babbled, suddenly realizing how safe I felt in my uncle's arms. How I had always felt that way, but that dumb Veronica Tucker steered me away with her ugly words. I vowed to myself to never let people convince me otherwise about how incredible he is.

"Dakota, do you remember what I told you in the hospital?" I stared into his eyes, remaining quiet for him to tell me again. "Sometimes you have to do things that don't seem right at the time, but it's the only way to make it right."

I nodded and wiped my tears with the back of my hands.

"Dakota, I didn't know. I didn't know I had a son. His mother knew and maneuvered his internship. My only encounter with the woman was one night. That's all it takes, so be careful, Dakota. Okay?" he softly reminded me.

"Okay," was all I said as we let go. I wasn't about to explain my method of birth control.

"When he walked into my law firm, it was like I was looking in the mirror forty years ago," he confessed.

"Why didn't you tell me?" I asked.

"It wasn't the right time. Sorry you had to hear it from Veronica Tucker."

I nodded.

He gave me another squeeze while asserting, "I'm glad you understand and forgive me."

"Not so fast. You still have a lot of explaining to do, but not now... now I want you to meet," ... and with a French accent, I announced, "Pierre," gesturing him over.

Pierre moved slowly, looking irritated.

Don't tell me he'd read about my infamous uncle! I gave Gloria a quick 'what's-his problem?' look, but she only shrugged and smirked. Totally clueless.

"That's Peter in American — Wee?" Uncle Travis quipped.

Pierre forced a smirk, and I laughed at my uncle's attempt at 'yes' in French.

Then good ol' Betsy came around. Uncle Travis pulled her in. With his arms around her waist, he asked, "Peter, have you met my Betsy?" He didn't wait for an answer. "She's my girl...the prettiest waitress in all of Texas!"

Betsy smiled but then peeled off his hands and teased, "I'm going to be the poorest waitress in Texas if you don't let me go and do my job. We work on tips, you know."

My uncle smiled and swatted her butt as she scurried away to the table next to ours, where the patrons looked annoyed. I heard her apologize to them and then say, "Yup, that's him."

Great, more people who knew about my scandalous uncle. I told myself I mustn't care.

Pierre sat back down. And within minutes, Betsy brought around waters, beers, two Shirley Temples — one for Savannah and the other for Amber Lee, a Pepsi for me, and at least five different appetizers we didn't order, but she had taken the liberty, remembering what we liked the last time.

"Any specials?" Pierre asked her.

"Yeah, me!" Betsy answered playfully as she placed a beer down in front of him, even though he didn't order one.

I noticed she wasn't bending down in front of Pierre to show off her cleavage as she had with my uncle. Maybe there was more to her flirting with my uncle. Was a relationship slowly evolving? I seriously did not get how a girl in her 20s could go with someone who was old enough to be her father!

Pierre didn't ask again. He let Gloria order for him.

"One Hungry Man coming up," Betsy sang. The meal consisted of ribs, fried chicken, sausage, baked beans, coleslaw, and cornbread.

When the entrees arrived, Pierre asked timidly, as if he were afraid of Betsy, "Are there any greens with this?"

She stared at him, then the coleslaw on his plate.

"Please?" he added.

Betsy brought him a garden salad with French dressing, which he scraped off with his knife as best he could. Was French dressing one of those pretend French things we Americans made up, like challah French toast? Other than the coleslaw not passing as a vegetable and the French dressing, Pierre seemed pleased with everything else. He devoured the ribs — cleaned them to the bone.

We allowed Pierre to digest his meal a little before we pulled him onto the dance floor for line dancing. Uncle Travis even let him don his cowboy hat. It's remarkable what a few shots of Wild Turkey can do. Then came the mechanical bull. Pierre was a trouper and really gave it his all until he was thrown off at the thirty-six-second mark. Rhonda's had an enormous timer that lit up like a Christmas tree against the planked wall. Luke, Gloria, and I had a go, and then it was time to leave. Even with the upbeat, rowdy music booming, Savannah and Amber Lee looked sleepy. Uncle Travis stayed and waited for Betsy's shift to end. He said he'd come by in the morning to talk and sort things out with me.

Chapter 34

Sunflower

"AS ALWAYS, we have a blast together!" Gloria said as she hugged me goodbye. "I'm so glad we got to see each other before heading to college. Thanks for convincing Luke to have Pierre come, too. You do realize Amber Lee is going to cook French for the next week or so — Pierre wrote down a ton of his family's recipes for her."

"Oy!" I said, in the best Yiddish voice I could.

Gloria laughed and gave my shoulders a tight squeeze as I walked her out to her dad's BMW. Mr. Gold was overseas on business, so she was able to use his car.

"I'll just have to work off those sticks of butter the French bathe their food in!" I said, patting my stomach as if it were already bloated.

"Yeah, with Cooper," Gloria teased. "Good ol' sexercise!"

I had no rebuttal. Sex was one subject I wanted to stay clear of with Gloria — comparing and contrasting Cooper in bed. No thank you! Luckily there wasn't any room for an awkward silence because Savannah came running out.

"Goria! Goria!" Savannah bellowed. "I got something for you!" She held up the wet painting. It was of a giant sunflower with big eye-lashed eyes and a smiling face. Red hearts floated against a turquoise blue sky, acting as clouds. "Do you like it?" she asked, looking so proud.

"No. I don't like it. I love it!" Gloria cried, "It's absolutely Boo — Ta — Full!"

Savannah giggled. "The picture's of me!"

"Of course — I can see the resemblance!" Gloria teased, holding up the picture close to Savannah's face as some paint slowly dripped down. "Oops," Gloria said as she quickly turned the damp paper flat in her hands and continued flattering Savannah, whose eyes twinkled brighter than the sun. "This is going to be the first thing I hang on my walls in my dorm room! I absolutely love it!" Then Gloria carefully handed me the painting so she could pick Savannah up. She gave her a loud kiss on her rosy cheek and told her again how much she loved the painting. "More than all the chocolate ice cream in the whole wide world!"

Savannah looked wowed, as if she was picturing endless bowls of chocolate ice cream.

I carefully laid the painting on the floor in the back of the car and told Gloria, "It should be completely dry by the time you get home, but just in case any gets on the Beemer, it's water-based and should come off easily with a sponge and soapy water, so not to worry. We only buy non-toxic and stain-resistant for our little Picasso."

Pierre gave me and Savannah two pecks goodbye as he climbed into the passenger side. Gloria had plopped herself behind the wheel.

"Buckle up. Drive safe," I reminded her as I closed her door. She put down the window for one last goodbye.

"Thanks again, and when I get settled, I'll call you." She slowly pulled away, and before she reached the turn-around, she blew me one last kiss, calling out, "Bye. Love you!" and beeped the horn.

Savannah continued to wave until the sedan was out of sight. "Can we make cookies and send them to her, pease?"

"Absolutely, but let's wait one week. I don't know her address at college yet."

"Can we make cookies for us?"

"What kind?" I asked as we headed back inside.

Chapter 35

And The Truth...

WHEN DISNEY'S *The Fox and the Hound* was nearing the end, I could hear my uncle's car come to a stop in our driveway. He had finally arrived at our house after spending the night and morning with Betsy. I peered down at Savannah's face and saw she had fallen asleep. Her head was resting on my lap, so I carefully slid out from under her and replaced my lap with one of the throw pillows on the sofa. Luke and Amber Lee had left to run a few errands at the start of the movie, and I told them to take advantage of my being home to watch Savannah, so why not go out to eat. Amber Lee became ecstatic at the suggestion and told Luke about this restaurant that had an enormous buffet. I laughed, picturing Amber Lee's third plate piled high. I made my way to the kitchen, knowing Uncle Travis would be coming through the back door. I had read another disturbing article in the paper about the ongoing investigation of Jake Jennings' suicide, and what I wanted to ask my uncle was weighing heavily on my mind. I hadn't really paid attention to the movie because I was inwardly rehearsing what I wanted to say to him. I knew I had to remain calm with him. He had a short fuse.

"Hey, Uncle Travis! So did you attend Betsy's spin class this time?" I teased.

"I gave her my own version of spin class," he chuckled as he placed his briefcase on one of the stools. It was bursting with loose papers and files — no wonder he couldn't zip it closed. He saw my glance and added, "I've got a lot of work to do today, and I think my chances of getting it done here are greater than at Betsy's. She's insatiable."

I put up my hand and cried, "Save it. I don't want to hear about your sex life!"

"You started it!" he retorted, sticking out his tongue.

"My mother always said you were a child in adult form — now I know what she meant!"

"I'm starvin'!"

"There's some leftover coq au vin," I answered in a French accent.

My uncle whispered, bending closer to me, his breath reeking of a hangover, "Has the Frenchman left?"

I whispered back loudly, "Oui, monsieur."

"Oh, good. He was an oddball," he said in his regular voice.

I chuckled at my uncle's reference. "What makes you say that?"

He winced. "He just looked uncomfortable."

"He did try the mechanical bull," I said, defending Pierre in his absence. Something my father always did if an ill word was said about someone behind his back, although my uncle was right — it was like Pierre didn't fit his own skin.

"Yes, but only after I fed him three shots of Wild Turkey did he even consider the bull. He climbed on after shot four!"

"Lucky for us, he didn't puke. That would've been disgusting."

"Eww!" He winced like a small child, then walked over to the fridge and pulled out a Fresca. "Wouldn't put him and Gloria together. How'd they meet?"

"He was placed with the Golds through their temple — some foreign exchange program."

My uncle nodded.

I prodded, "Do you think she and Cooper looked better suited?"

"Doesn't matter. They're not together anymore," he stated matter-of-factly and chugged his soda.

"No, really. Tell me. I can take it," I urged.

"Ah…that's good!" he sighed, then took a seat at the kitchen island. He saw I was serious — still waiting for his opinion, looking pensive with my arms folded. "Dakota, it doesn't matter what I think."

"I hate when you do that."

"Do what?"

"Skirt the issue," I barked.

"Dakota, if you're asking for my approval — if I think you and Cooper should go out — if you should marry him someday…way, way down the road, I would still tell you the same answer. Doesn't matter what I think. You're the one sharing your life with him, and vice versa. It's your decision, not mine."

"Hmm. Okay. But tell me why you don't like him."

"Who? Pierre or Cooper?" he asked, pretending to be thick in the head.

I threw the oven mitt at him. "Bernard Travis Kenwood, if you want to eat, you better quit toying with me and answer me honestly. I deserve that."

"Oh, you're serious. Well then. Miss Dakota Summer Buchannan. FDA approved!" he said, stamping the counter with his fist.

"Very funny," I smirked.

"However," he started, without relenting his fist, "I don't like how Cooper was behind that ditsy columnist, Veronica Tucker — helping her with her…" He hesitated as if he was lost for words, "reporting. I guess that's what you'd call it. But her facts were all jumbled."

"They went out," I volunteered, and he didn't seem surprised in the least. It was like he knew.

"I don't care who she slept with, but the fact is Cooper was with you when all this was coming to a head, and he should have told her off."

"You're right," I said. And I meant it. My uncle had a valid point, and I began thinking about being upset at Cooper — again! Geez, it seemed like we got into tiffs way more than I did with Hubbell.

"Unless it was his way of getting back at me. And honestly, since you asked for my honest opinion, I believe he enjoyed all the dirt she was digging up on me — to get back at me for defending Willet Mathews and getting him off on manslaughter. Cooper loves you. He didn't want to hurt you. He wanted to hurt me. But what he didn't realize was his hurting me hurt you. But I think now he realizes this." He took my hand and held it, looking into my eyes, and reminded me, "He's bent on finding a reason for tragically losing his parents when there'll never be one. It was an accident, Dakota, just like your dad's death was an accident."

Since he was being honest, I blurted out, "Was Jake Jennings' suicide an accident?"

"What?" he immediately sounded annoyed. "How the hell am I supposed to know that, Dakota?"

"I read another article this morning in the paper, saying there were two highball glasses found on his bar in his penthouse, so he wasn't alone."

"It's a bar, Dakota. I'm sure he had more than two glasses."

"Used." Now I was getting annoyed with him trying to play dumb. "The melted ice cubes showed remnants of whiskey and soda water. Wild Turkey, to be exact."

"Are you implying I was with Jake Jennings the night he jumped off his balcony?" His voice grew angrier. "You should know by now I drink it straight."

I could feel tears begin to well, but managed to say, "He was drunk; that's what the autopsy report revealed."

"Your point?"

"Whoever he was with could have pushed him."

"Or the person he was with had already left. Jennings had a reputation as a mean drunk."

"So it was an accident. He stumbled on his own balcony and fell over?"

"I told you, Dakota. How am I supposed to know?"

"The article made Jake sound 'normal,' not suicidal," I cried.

"Unless he had a dark secret and drinking made it worse...and in a drunken stupor, he ended his life. Subconsciously, he decided he couldn't live with himself any longer."

I remained silent, staring at my uncle. Where was he going with this?

"You've never heard the saying, 'The demon got the best of him'?" he asked.

"Inner demons? Yeah, I've heard of it. Seen it in horror movies. So you believe it was a suicide?"

My uncle just nodded.

"But where's the usual suicide note?"

"Maybe he was too drunk to write one. Maybe he didn't want people to know of this secret; if there was one."

"Let's say the secret was that he really did cause my dad's death. But why?" I began to cry. "What did my dad do to him that could make him want to kill him?"

"Dakota, numerous investigations have proven that there was a mechanical malfunction in the air compressor of the machine your dad happened to be working with when it finally blew. It could have been any worker. Your dad, unfortunately, was the one. Your dad's death was an accident."

"So what do you suppose this 'big dark secret' you're talking about is that made Jake kill himself?" I cried.

"I don't know. Nobody knows yet. I heard that detectives are searching his parents' home, where he grew up."

"For clues? They're thinking it stems from childhood?" I asked, completely taken aback.

"But don't repeat that. I shouldn't have told you." He sounded regretful that he'd divulged that piece of information to me.

I did what I always seem to do when faced with uncertainty — I cry. I hid my face in my hands, leaning over the counter. Uncle Travis stood up, leaned over, and gently peeled my hands away. He looked into my eyes and calmly said, "You don't need to worry anymore, Dakota. Whatever was eating Jake Jennings is done with. He's in a better place. He didn't kill your dad, rest assured."

I nodded, still sniveling.

"And he obviously wasn't normal if he held you captive, so whoever wrote that article is just plain stupid. Jennings was definitely nearing his breaking point. If it weren't for that old busybody neighbor, Mrs. Turner, he might have killed you that night. She saved you. And as uncanny as it may sound, killing himself is what saved him…"

"From his inner demons," I finished.

"That's right." He sighed and sat back down. He looked exhausted but relieved, as if some weight had been lifted from him. He told me, "Come here."

I came around the kitchen island. He drew me in for a hug.

"I love you so much, Dakota. You're like a daughter to me." He kissed the top of my head.

We released our hold, and, facing each other, my uncle tenderly confided, "Dakota, when your mama was dying, you know what she told me?" He didn't expect me to answer. "She told me," he sighed and looked as if he was the one now trying to hold back tears. He repeated, "She told me to 'take care of my baby girl. Help Jethro make her into an independent woman — God knows we need more of them.'"

I chuckled. It was totally something my mother would say.

"Dakota, that's just what I'm trying to do. I'm here for you, with whatever you need. And I'll always protect you."

I nodded. "I know that, Uncle Travis. I love you, too. You're like a father to me."

He smiled. "Good, we're back on the same page. But let's return to our initial conversation about Cooper."

I blushed.

"Darlin', I'm here for you, with whatever you need, but when it comes to someone who you're intimate with, I can't tell you whether it's right or wrong. Only you know that." He gently took my hand and placed it on my own heart, and said, "It's what you feel right here."

I smiled at his poetic gesture.

He smiled. "But I can tell you this. Your mama wanted you to finish college before belonging to a man. So just remember you have four years ahead of you, and they all belong to you. Not anybody else! Okay, Miss Dakota Summer Buchannan?"

"Okay," I said and returned the formality with a smile. "I'll do my very best, Mr. Bernard Travis Kenwood."

And just then, the oven timer went off. Savannah ran into the kitchen with as many markers as she could hold in both her hands and bellowed, "What's cookin'?"

"You are, good-lookin'!" my uncle cried, capturing her and plopping her down on his lap, "Miss Savannah, did you know you are just the sweetest little girl in the whole wide world?"

Savannah giggled, and I smiled, remembering him acting the same way with me when I was about her age. And just then, I was reminded again how truly blessed I was.

Savannah playfully pleaded, "Put me down! I want to color!"

He did, and she scurried off in search of paper. He excused himself to go to the bathroom before eating Amber Lee's leftover coq au vin, so I was left to reflect and ponder.

Even with my parents gone, I was never left alone. I was genuinely loved and looked after, and this made it easier for me to forgive. Quoting the prolific Paul Boese: "Forgiveness does not change the past, but it does enlarge the future." I forgave my uncle. I forgave Cooper, and, believe it or not, I even forgave Jake Jennings. I don't mean to sound pious for also realizing that life is too short — too short to be holding grudges or animosity and letting it eat away at your soul. Naturally, life will have storms you have to weather. Just like the period of grieving melts away after someone you love passes but the fond memories you cherish will always remain with you and sustain you. Primarily, my days were full of sunshine, regardless of the actual weather, and I knew I had plenty of time to explore the many possibilities with an open mind and an open heart.

But just as fast as lightning strikes and the damage it can do in a matter of seconds takes hold, my pleasant moment was shattered when Savannah held up a picture she had drawn. She cheerfully called, "Look, Aunt Dakota, at what I made for Uncle Travis." The light poured through the paper. Words were written on the opposite side. She had drawn on the back of what looked like a letter. Signed by Jake Jennings.

Acknowledgments

THANK YOU to my wonderful friends who read the very first draft of *Dakota* and loved it! You know who you are. ;) Your enthusiasm and sound advice was priceless.

Thank you to the director of Histria Books, Kurt Brackob. Your kind words, sound advice, and "directions" were perfect.

Thank you to my editor Sheila Grimes whose edits and suggestions were quintessential.

My gratitude extends to the rest of the Histria team who have helped form this book and are continuing to promote it. I feel privileged to be one of your authors.

And last, but certainly not least, a ginormous shout out to the fans of my debut novel, *Because of Savannah*, who have eagerly asked about its sequel. I thank you so much for your patience and support. I hope this finds you well and *Dakota* meets all your expectations.

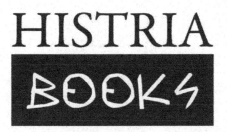
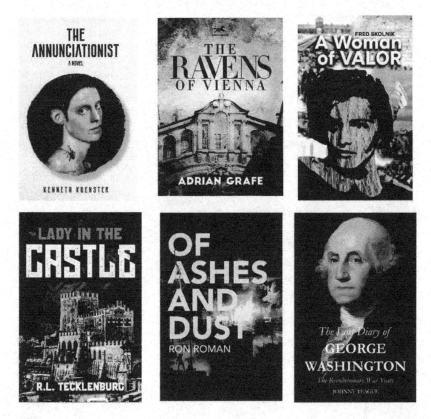